Farrar · Straus · Giroux)   *New York*

Tell me that you love me, Junie Moon

MARJORIE KELLOGG

With an Introduction by Paula Fox

FOR MOTHER AND SKIP

About Junie Moon

When Marjorie Kellogg and I
first met in the early forties, we were both very young and
broke. Something my father had told me suggested a way
we might earn some money. In those days, "true" story
magazines crammed the racks in the candy stores. Their
pages were filled with tales about the peril and delight of
romance. The heroines were pretty, innocent young women
who, in the course of pursuing their careers (secretarial),
met handsome young men (the boss), fell in love with them,
gave their all, and then discovered these fellows were already
married, fatally ill, or else were simply cads. Wiser and
sadder, the young women gave up their worldly ambitions
and returned to home towns where true love (the druggist's
son as often as not) had been patiently waiting all the time.

Sometimes, perhaps to make the stories "true," the young women got into serious trouble.

In any event, my father had told me that the stories were not written by pretty, innocent young women but by impecunious writers trying to earn a dollar. The magazines paid three or four cents a word; it looked like an easy way to make some money. Marjorie and I invested in an armful of them, read them through, and resolved to try our hands. It was not to be. We could manage a rough plot and a first line, "On a bright day in October, Nora was driving down Riverside Drive when—" and then we would begin to contrive such preposterous and ribald variations on the one or two story "lines" suggested by our reading that we were undone by laughter. We kept at it a month or so, then gave up.

We both got jobs and went our separate ways, but we always kept in touch and years later collaborated on a television script for an afternoon series which, to our astonishment, sold. But we each had another kind of writing in mind, and in due time we both got to it.

In 1968, when Junie Moon made her first appearance with her "torn, disfigured face"—a face like a "jack-o'-lantern"—she created a great stir. She was not a pretty innocent; she knew love was hard, hard to get and hard to give, and that it was not the exclusive province of handsome people.

Life has cut Junie Moon every which way. She has no interest in the surface look of people; she knows about the vulnerable bones beneath the flesh. She knows how, and often why, people suffer, and she doesn't turn away from them because they suffer. She is bountiful yet tough-minded, and it is these qualities in her that make her so attractive to anyone whose life she touches, so attractive that they begin not to see her wounded face and hands, or, as Junie remarks herself, she began to forget what people looked like "because her feelings washed over their features and changed them as the tide changes sand."

This story, which starts so simply—"Once there were three patients who met in the hospital and decided to live together"—reminds Marjorie Kellogg's readers of the startling pleasures and charm of commonplace events and things which are so easily forgotten—of lemonade and chocolate brownies at critical moments, of the smell and feel of the beach, the ocean, of the mysterious and imponderable ways of a smart dog, of the healing sympathy between people, the freedom of sleeping on a cot in the open air, of the perverse joy of familiar arguments between old friends, of a "rundown bungalow under an oppressive tree," which has a window into which wild roses have grown.

The patients, "three freaks, one, a female," carry out their intention to live together, and as one of them, Warren, a paraplegic, observes, "There have been worse plans made in the world."

Like most plans, it doesn't entirely work out. But while it is working, their lives are illuminated by the dominant quality in Junie Moon's temperament—her sunniness. It is sunniness in a harsh landscape; it takes you by surprise, it is a bird singing on the branch of a blasted tree, but sunniness and song it is.

The story of these three, Junie and Warren, and Arthur, who has a progressive neurological disease, reminds me of other stories—J. D. Salinger's *The Catcher in the Rye*, and Carson McCullers's *The Member of the Wedding*, to name two—stories which have the power, as the Quakers say, to speak to one's condition.

Junie and her friends are outsiders. They have been ravaged by disease and their fellow man, and woman, and the results of it show. Most of us can hide our wounds, unconfessed secrets, or we can group together and assert that we are not outsiders—all those other people are.

It seems to me that for young readers who must experience the bafflement and uncertainty and frequent mortifications which attend growing up, this book can be especially compelling and comforting, and might even help anneal the pain of the conflict between the wish to be different and the horrid suspicion that one is *too* different.

How I longed, when young, to sink into what I imagined was the anonymity of being like everyone else! But who was, who is, everyone else?

Marjorie Kellogg tells us who three people are, and what they are like, and how they try to live together and how they try to care about each other. In doing so the way she has, with charity for human weakness, and hope in a human, and humane, capacity to survive, she suggests that other people are only variations on a simple ineluctable *one*, the person each of us is, and that everyone else is, too.

—*Paula Fox*

Tell me that you love me, Junie Moon

 *One*

Once there were three patients who met in the hospital and decided to live together. They arrived at this decision because they had no place to go when they were discharged.

Despite the fact that these patients often quarreled and nagged each other, and had, so far as they knew, nothing in common, they formed an odd balance—like three pawnshop balls.

The first patient was called Warren. When he was seventeen, he and a friend were out hunting rabbits when the friend's gun went off and the bullet struck Warren in the middle of his spine. From then on he was paraplegic and spent the rest of his days in a wheelchair.

The second patient was Arthur. He had a progressive

neurological disease which no one had been able to diagnose. He estimated that he had been asked to touch his finger to his nose 6,012 times, and he could recite the laboratory findings on himself for the past five years, in case the doctors wanted them reviewed. Arthur walked with a careening gait and his hands fluttered about his face like butterflies.

The third patient was a woman named Junie Moon. That was her real name. An irate man had beaten her half to death in an alley one night and had topped off his violence by throwing acid over her. She had a number of pitiful and pesky deformities.

The idea of their living together originated with Warren. He was fat and lazy and did not relish the thought of being alone or looking after himself. He was also a cheerful organizer of other people's time and affairs and could paint lovely pictures of how things would be later on.

"My dear friends," he said to Arthur and Junie Moon one night after the evening medications had been given out, "I have a solution to our collective dilemma." Junie Moon, who was playing checkers with Arthur in the far end of the corridor, scowled at Warren from her torn, disfigured face.

"With the various pittances we could collect from this and that source," Warren went on, as Arthur inadvertently knocked two checkers on the floor, "we could live fairly comfortably." Warren retrieved the checkers and patted Arthur on the shoulder. "What do you think?"

"Nobody wants to live with me," Junie Moon said, "so shut up about it."

"I think the idea stinks," Arthur said, as his hand flew into the air.

Then he and Junie Moon bent closer to the board as if to dismiss Warren's preposterous scheme.

"Don't pretend that either of you have a place to go," Warren said, leaning forward in his wheelchair so that his face was on a level with theirs, "because you haven't!" He gave Junie Moon a lascivious wink: "You'll end up at the old-ladies home and you know what goes on *there!*"

"At least it's better than nothing," she said. Her scarred mouth shifted painfully to permit a laugh. Warren was still not used to her face, but he loved her quick humor.

"But I'm better than a dozen old ladies," he said, "and more responsible."

"Baloney!" shouted Arthur, which set off a terrible spasm of his body and almost lifted him from his chair. Automatically, Warren and Junie Moon laid a hand on his shoulders to quiet him.

"You are many things," Arthur said when he had regained control of himself, "but responsible is not one of them."

"But he may be better than the poorhouse at that," Junie Moon said. "What do you have in mind?"

"Well now!" Warren reared back in his wheelchair and stroked his bright blond beard. He said: "We will each have our own room. Junie Moon will do the cooking. Arthur will go to the store. I can see it all now."

"And I can see you have planned nothing for yourself in the way of expended effort," Arthur said.

"Who in their right mind would rent us an apartment?" Junie Moon said. "Three freaks, one a female."

"We'll do it by phone," Warren said. "We'll say we're much too busy to come in person."

"When the landlord takes one look at us, he will throw us out," Junie Moon said.

"He couldn't," Arthur said. "We represent at least three different minority groups." By making this remark, Arthur had cast his vote in favor of the plan. Junie Moon held out a little longer.

"It's bad enough seeing the two of you in this hospital every day," she said, "let alone living with you."

At this, the men banded together and attacked her.

"You're no prize yourself," Warren said.

"And you probably have a lot of disgusting personal habits of which we are not aware and to which you will expose us once we agree to a common arrangement," Arthur said.

"Let's not talk about prizes," Junie Moon said to Warren. "If we did, you might take the cake."

Arthur, who was the more sensitive of the two men, realized by something in Junie Moon's voice that they had hurt her feelings. Because her face was so disfigured, it was difficult to read her emotions.

"I suppose none of us would take a prize," Arthur said. "On the other hand, we have a few things in our favor, I believe." He turned his head abruptly so the other two could not see him blush over this self-compliment.

"What are you three up to?" Miss Oxford, the chief nurse, asked, looking thin and suspicious.

"We are plotting your demise," Warren said cheerfully. Miss Oxford scurried away, glancing over her shoulder.

Junie Moon then decided to join the two men in their plan. "I've thought of a number of ways to get that nurse," she said. "We must try a few of them before we leave here to set up housekeeping."

That was the way they decided.

 *Two*

Junie Moon had been a stringy child and a stringier young woman. She loped along instead of walking, and she made jokes to cover up her lack of beauty. No one wanted to marry her until she was twenty-five, and then there came a long procession of men asking for her hand—men who were failures, or who were as ugly as she, or who were running away from something. Most of them were shifty-eyed and came from such places as Oklahoma or Tacoma, Washington. One after the other, Junie Moon turned them away. Her mother, sad that Junie Moon had not married and moved out, would look after the men as they went off down the steps and say: "I couldn't see what was wrong with *that* one."

Once in a while Junie Moon would go with one of them

to the beach or to the drive-in, but she disliked their sour smell and the way they thought they could feel her leg ten minutes after they met her. After a while, she gave up going out—that is until Jesse came along. Jesse wore greasy black pants and a lilac-colored T-shirt. He smelled as though he didn't own any other clothes, but he had a kind of style about him that she had missed in the others. He would sit on the edge of the couch and look directly at her mother and father when they were speaking, and from time to time he would talk to her in a special way that made her spine tingle. He seemed to know something about everything, but he never spoke a word about his background or his mother or his brothers, if he had any.

Then one night Jesse drove her out to the edge of town and told her to undress behind an abandoned roadside stand. She didn't like this idea and she told him so, but the look that came onto his face scared her half to death, so she complied. She stood there in the stubble field behind the shed with her skinny legs bent together and her long arms wrapped around her chest while Jesse sat on the ground and recited a long list of obscenities. After about half an hour he told her to get dressed and they started back to town.

Junie Moon's mistake was that on the way back she got to thinking about how she must have looked standing there naked as a bird with a big grown man sitting at her feet, and the thought made her laugh. She laughed so hard she didn't see Jesse's face contort into a terrible, mean look. She was still laughing when he pulled her out of the car, dragged her down the alley next to the A & P, and beat her half to death. She lay there for a long time—long enough at least for him to find a bottle of acid and come back and fix her up altogether. They never caught Jesse for his terrible crime although they put out a four-state alarm for him.

After that, Junie Moon lay in the hospital for a long time. They had her in a room by herself at first because she had gotten pneumonia and almost died. Her eyes were bandaged up and so were her ears, and there was a hole left for her mouth. When people talked to her, they leaned close to this dark hole and shouted as if her ears were there. She could feel their breath on her teeth, but their voices were far away, filtered out by the heavy layers of gauze. When she got well enough to eat by mouth, a nurse would sit by the bed and poke various smashed foods into her. The nurses did not like to do this, and as a result they rushed to get it over with, making a mess of things and ending up getting angry with her. She found that when the nurses said, "Let's eat our dinner like a good girl," she wanted very much to hit them in the face. She was unable to do this, however, because her right arm was in a cast with a nasty, splintered break, and her left arm was being used for a skin graft and was strapped to the side of her throat. She remained this way for eight weeks and then was moved to another floor where there were men as well as women and where patients were sent to get rehabilitated. Junie Moon thought this was a big joke. "I've never been habilitated," she said, "let alone re."

Warren was raised by a group of writers who went to Provincetown in the summer and lived in various big cities during the winter. He was born during the Depression to a pretty girl of sixteen. She had come to Provincetown from Boston with her father, who was an architect, and her mother, who was a biochemist, both of whom were very liberal-minded people. When their daughter became pregnant by one or the other of the writers, they tried not to act surprised, though if the truth were known, they were aghast, both of them. The writers discussed the matter with the young girl and her parents in a very honest and gentlemanly way, with the result that they decided that she should have the baby and they would all take care of it. They drew up lists and charts (some in color) of a "Rotation Child-Care Plan" designed to share the burden of Warren's care among them, but the plan did not survive two winters and the burden eventually fell to Warren's grandmother and a young man named Guiles who lived in New York and who worked in a handbag factory. Guiles was the ex-boyfriend of one of the original writers. He kept the baby in the wintertime although it took most of his salary to hire a woman during the day. He would rush home from work, having now found a reason to live, with a bag of food under one arm and a library book, which he had gotten during the noon hour, under the other. He first questioned the hired woman carefully as to the events of the day—did the baby eat, did he take his nap?—then he would question her again, and then again to make sure there were no inconsistencies. His obsessiveness caused many a woman to leave the job, but Guiles was fortunate in always finding another. After the woman would leave for the day, Guiles would perch Warren on his hip while he cooked supper for the two of them. He found that Warren liked egg noodles, tuna, limes and toasted cinnamon buns in particular, and strawberry Jello with apricots occasionally. After supper, Guiles would hold the baby in his lap and read to him. Before Warren was three, he had heard a great deal of Melville, some Hemingway, Dorothy Parker, Sinclair Lewis, and bits and pieces of James Joyce, as well as *The Conquest of Mexico*. In the morning, Guiles would bathe him to the tune of the only phonograph record he owned: *Divertissement* by Ibert. Apparently Warren enjoyed this because he would laugh and beat on the surface of the bath water with his fists.

Each Fourth of July weekend, Guiles would take the baby on the train to Boston, where he would be met by Warren's grandmother, the biochemist. She returned him after Labor Day, brown and healthy, but rather serious-looking.

When Warren was seven, Guiles was hit by a delivery truck and died on his way to the hospital. Fortunately for Warren, Guiles had posted a notice above the sink in his apartment which said in case of emergency Warren's grandmother was to be notified. The poor woman came the next day and packed Warren off to Boston. He was pale and depressed for almost ten months, but finally he began to come around. His grandmother spoke to him a great deal about Guiles, having Warren believe that Guiles was his father. She made Guiles out to be much stronger and romantic than he really was. Warren knew this was not true, but he loved Guiles for his own reasons and he did not argue with his grandmother. It took some doing, but he managed to preserve some accurate memories of the thin little man who perched him on his hip while he prepared the tuna fish.

When he was seventeen, Warren went out on the Provincetown dunes with his buddy Melvin Coffee to shoot rabbits. Instead, Melvin shot him in the back. They both agreed to say that it had been an accident.

Arthur was a perfectly normal, healthy individual until he was twelve. Then he developed a weakness in his right hand. This made him drop things: first his chocolate cup at the breakfast table. Then his schoolbooks began to fall out of his hand and splatter over the sidewalk. One hot afternoon in May he was sitting in his social-studies class when he felt himself beginning to fall as though he had been thrown into a deep pit. When he woke up, he was on the classroom floor and a wooden ruler was between his teeth.

Arthur's mother's irritation turned to worry when, instead of outgrowing his symptoms, he seemed to get worse. He could hear his parents talking long into the night about his fits and other distressing symptoms. He was frightened because their quarreling, which he had grown used to through the years, suddenly stopped when they spoke of him. It made him want to run away from home, but he could not think where to go. He was taken instead to thirty-five different hospitals and clinics.

When Arthur was eighteen, his mother gave up on him and took him off to a state school for the feeble-minded. Then she and Arthur's father moved away from the town and never came back. At first the shock of the babbling and drooling and stench of the institution almost killed him. Then the authorities set him to work in the vegetable fields and things were better. Three years later he ran away. He still had no place to go, but he went back to town and got a job as a messenger boy. Sometimes Arthur would sit in his furnished room over the Majestic Theater and worry about what was to become of him. The strength of his left leg was beginning to slip away and he walked as though he were on a pitching ship.

"We will demonstrate the virtues of collectivism," Arthur said to Warren and Junie Moon. "My experience in the institution may be of some help after all."

"The feeble-minded can teach us all a trick or two," said Warren.

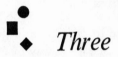 *Three*

An orderly had overheard their plan to live together and by the next morning staff and patients alike were discussing it.

"I think it's fantastic. Fantastic," Miss Oxford, the chief nurse, said as she popped the medications into tiny paper cups.

"Well, *I* think it's great," Miss Holt, her assistant, said.

"Your problem is that you tend to identify with the rebellious element," Miss Oxford said.

"Your problem," Miss Holt said, "is that you attend too many psych seminars. If you would spend the time in more sinful pursuits, things would be a lot easier around here."

She stormed off and Miss Oxford made a note to discuss

professional deportment, as it concerned the use of immoral-
ity, with Miss Holt.

"Freaksville!" young John Goren said when he learned of
the plan. "Don't it just get you where you live?" Goren had
grown as mean as fire since the accident which cut off his
leg.

In the opposite bed Ted Porter groaned. "Why don't you
take your damned sick humor and shove it!" Ted was usually soft and gentle-spoken, but his nerves were rubbed raw
by his own perplexing medical problem and the loud mouth
of young Goren.

"Why don't *you* join the freak brigade?" Goren hissed.
"It seems to me you'd make the perfect fourth."

Ted tried to raise up on his elbow. Had he been able to do
so, he would have then tried to rap Goren in the mouth.

"Hey!" It was Miss Holt. She had a way of jumping into
the middle of trouble and smoothing it out without anybody
getting hurt. "Easy, easy." Her voice was soft.

Ted liked to look at her. It was the only thing about being
in the hospital that he could tolerate. He liked her long
hands and wished that he could paint them. Or hold them.
He liked the merry way she looked at patients which diluted
the heavy sick air over their beds. If it were possible to have
two wives, he certainly would have chosen Miss Holt to be
his second. One for loving, one for nursing, he thought. And
then, since there was always so much time, Ted composed
endless dreams about his life with two women. Some of
them made him smile.

"What do you think of those three setting up housekeeping?" Goren asked Miss Holt.

"Interesting idea," she said.

Goren's face was twisted with scorn. "Look, each one of them is bad enough by himself. Why do they want to make it worse by living together?"

"You sound like they asked you to join them," she said, rolling up his bed so he could look out to the mountains.

"Me! Are you kidding? You think I haven't got any place better to go?"

Miss Holt did not answer.

"Well, I have got some place to go, two or three places if you must know!"

She put her long, soothing hand on the back of his neck. In a minute he began to quiet down, but he was fighting back the tears which threatened his eyes.

"Shit!" he muttered.

"You're absolutely right," Miss Holt said.

The thought of a home made Arthur giddy with excitement. To him it meant being away in the daytime and coming back when it was getting dark into a yellow lighted kitchen which smelled of warm, comforting things to eat. He had not experienced this—his own mother had hated cooking and got through the meals as quickly as possible with the least amount of effort—but he had read about it in books. He also read of families who gathered in the parlor around the piano and sang or played musical instruments. As he thought about Warren's plan, he pictured the three of them in a small, neat cottage in the country. The more he thought of it, the more it began to look like a dream house—a turned-down thatched roof, flowers beside a winding path, and friendly smoke coming from the chimney.

> *"Day will break,*
> *And you'll awake,*
> *In time to bake*
> *A sugar cake . . ."*

Arthur tried to keep time as he sang, but his legs tangled with spasms and his heavy shoes chattered on the floor . . .

> *"For me to take*
> *For all the boys to seeeeeee . . ."*

"Oh Jesus," said Goren, "now it's trying to sing."

Since they were a league now, Arthur and Warren and Junie Moon, it was Junie Moon who knifed in like a swallow before the wind.

"Never mind with your mean remarks," she hissed at Goren. "You couldn't carry a tune in a bedpan." She shrieked at her own joke and loped off down the corridor, whacking Arthur on the back as she passed him.

Arthur persisted with his dream. In the back of the cottage was a stream which led into a dark forest. They would clear a space there and set up a croquet game to play on hot summer evenings. Junie Moon would wear a white dress and he and Warren would wear bright vests with softly knotted ties.

Would you like something cool to drink? Their voices were as soft as fireflies. Tell us about the time the feed store caught on fire. Well, it was about nine-thirty in the morning and Mr. Breck was in the back room when . . . Are you sure you wouldn't like something cool to drink? Tell us about the time the side show came to town. Well, one day late in the summer three old trucks stopped alongside of the fair grounds. When they opened the doors, you never saw so many freaks in your life. . . .

After a while it would grow completely dark and they would all go inside.

 *Four*

Warren began cutting pictures out of magazines. Guiles had taught him to do this. Make a little scrapbook, Guiles had said, and then you'll have something to look back on. He and Guiles made scrapbooks of Fish; Men's Shoes Through the Ages; and the Lesser Antilles Islands, among other things. Guiles said the effort of cutting and pasting fixed things in your mind.

From the magazines Warren could find on the ward—things like *Life* and *The Resident Physician*—he clipped examples of modern interior decoration. He particularly liked living rooms with "conversational groupings."

"How do you like this conversational grouping?" he asked Junie Moon, feeling compelled to clear with the lady of the house-to-be.

"Terrible!" she would say, without even looking. "Disgusting. You have the taste of a Hungarian fisherman."

"But it *lends* itself. It says right here: 'This unique grouping lends itself.' "

"That's a terrible sofa," snorted Junie Moon. "Give me an old-fashioned one any day. With sturdy legs. Danish modern is for Danish ladies with fat behinds. I, to the contrary, have thin flanks, and welcome the comfort of overstuffing!" Her raw face turned purple with emphasis. "Now what do you think of *this* conversational grouping?" she shouted, throwing Warren's scrapbook into the air.

Living with this impossible, wretched woman will never work, Warren thought. He had made a mistake to invite her into the plan. Instead he should have asked only Arthur and let it go at that. It would be easier in many ways with just Arthur. In the first place, Arthur looked quite normal if he stood perfectly still and could keep from having a spasm. When they got out of the hospital, Warren would encourage him to get a different haircut and use one of the new hair lotions he had seen advertised on television. If his hair could be made to look less like assorted bundles of dark straw, his general appearance would improve. Warren would also see to it that Arthur wore something other than printed short-sleeved shirts, which made his dark hairy arms look thin and wasted. Anyway, it was better with two men. They could sit in front of the fire with a glass of port and talk sensibly. They could eat when they felt like it and not be bound by womanish rules and regulations. And they could have young secretaries for dinner and other things. He would tell Junie Moon tomorrow that the deal was off.

In addition to his collection of living-room groupings, Warren also clipped pictures of kitchens. He preferred large kitchens where one could watch and the other could cook and he liked the oven to have a glass window. In Boston, where Warren went to live with his grandmother after Guiles was killed, there was a large cool kitchen in the rear of the house. Warren often studied his lessons there while the cook hummed to herself and cooked supper. On Saturdays he was allowed to make brownies and something he invented called hot yellow cake. His favorite procedure was mixing the butter and sugar until it became like a frothy icing, but the problem was adding the other ingredients before it disappeared.

"You're going to taste those brownies to death," the cook would say. Actually, he didn't like the taste too much after the chocolate was added—it was the consistency that appealed to him, tough and chewy.

"Lordy, lordy," Junie Moon cried, looking at Warren's kitchen pictures. "Who do you have in mind to do the cheffing?"

So gross. So crass. It would be quite impossible to live with her, Warren thought.

"You've got a funny look on your face," she said, taking his chin in her hand in a hard pinch. "Your eyes look mean and distrustful."

At that moment he felt too pale to tell her she would not be living with him and Arthur.

"I read some place you see yourself in another's eyes," he said.

"Oh you did, did you. How one man could read so much trash is beyond me."

"There's a lot in this world that's beyond you," he said ruefully.

She looked at him through narrow, scarred lids.

"Don't plot anything behind my back. You're just the type to do it." She turned on her heel and left him.

It made Warren nervous the way she plugged into his mind with the directness of a switchboard operator. His grandmother, the biochemist, was something like that, but she had been more casual—perhaps absent-minded—about it.

Oh, by the way, his grandmother would say, you've probably been wondering . . . And then she would go straight to the heart of what he thought even though it was quite a secret and personal matter. Like one day when they were swimming together in a pond near Wellfleet. "Oh, by the way," she said, "you probably wonder about your mother when you come up here, don't you?" He was stunned and could only look at her with blank eyes. Only a moment before he was thinking about his mother, trying to imagine her face as he swam underwater, trying to place her in his vision among the reeds and currents.

"I don't wonder much," he had said to his grandmother.

"It's natural that you would," she said, not accepting his statement. "How much did Guiles tell you about her?"

"Not much," he said, diving out of her sight, out of the sound of her questions. As a matter of fact, Guiles had said a great deal. "And now we will talk about your mother," he would begin, in much the same way he would introduce *The Conquest of Mexico.* And Warren would lean against him on the couch or lie with his head in Guiles's lap and watch his chin move as he talked about Warren's mother.

"She was a lovely thing, as I recall." Guiles's voice grew husky, just right for recounting things from long ago. Warren saw a beautiful blond girl, tanned and laughing, running across the beach. The way Guiles told it, you could taste the salt on her skin, feel the warm sun as she ran beneath it. He would recount to Warren every detail he could remember—she wore an old army shirt and shorts most of the time, and once in a while a dress—usually a bright silk which would make her look so beautiful Guiles wanted to cry.

Being a sensitive person, Junie Moon smelled trouble in the air almost before Warren manufactured it. She was certain that Warren had changed his mind about them living together, or at least her living with them. In a way, she felt relieved. The thought of the three of them outside of the protective walls of the hospital was appalling to her. And the thought of she herself being seen by outsiders was one which she had postponed.

Minnie, who lay dying in the next bed, was the only one to mention it. They talked mostly at night while the others slept.

"He got you real bad, Junie Moon," Minnie said one night. Her voice sounded far away, like a lonely train going across the fields. "A man that would do a thing like that ought never to be born."

"I didn't think he was mean," Junie Moon said.

"I never knew a mean man who looked it," Minnie sighed. "It's the sweet baby-faced ones you got to step aside for. Did it hurt?"

"What?"

"When he poured on the acid."

She tried to remember. "A terrible stink, like something burning. I don't remember much about the pain. There was so much of it, it was like drinking too much—after a while everything gets fuzzy and in slow motion. Later it hurt. I'll tell you that for a fact."

"He sure got you real bad. Have you seen yourself?"

"Why should I go around looking at myself, can you tell me that?" She wanted to tell Minnie to mind her own damned business, but then she looked at the thin little woman, her hair in tiny pigtails all over her head, her abdomen full of tubes and drains and incisions. At last she said: "It was pretty bad."

Minnie's voice was almost a whisper. "Of course I didn't know you before, Junie Moon. You probably was a good-looking woman, that would be my guess."

"But now, Minnie?"

"Now it's like you say: pretty bad."

There. The words fell like stones. She did not think she could tolerate the sound. Later that night she went into the bathroom, bolted the door, and turned on the glaring overhead light. She walked straight to the mirror.

When she first saw herself, she tried to scream, but no sound came. She stood watching the horrible face in the mirror trying to scream, the mouth cavernous despite the fact that the lips could barely open. "Help," she cried soundlessly, "help." She moved her bottom jaw up and down and it reminded her of a marionette's mechanical mouth. "Help." No one came. The bathroom light seemed to get brighter. The crimson trench where the nose had been gave her face a bloody jack-o'-lantern look. It was worse than she had thought.

When she went to bed, Minnie was still awake, staring up at the ceiling.

"You went to look?" Minnie asked. Junie Moon didn't answer. "It won't ever be so bad as it was in there," Minnie said. Then she turned to Junie Moon. "Let Minnie see your hand. Come on now. I heard you smash the mirror." She took a towel from her nightstand and wrapped it around Junie Moon's bleeding hand. "No more blood for you, missy. The worst part is over."

"The hell you say, Minnie." It was hard to tell if Minnie heard or not. She was in and out of her dreams so much. And when she slept she talked as if she were awake.

Later that night Minnie cried: "Come and get me, I'm tired of waiting."

"Turn over, Minnie."

"I dreamed I was falling. Falling off a big mountain to the bottom of the sea."

"Turn over, Minnie."

"My mama wore a bright green dress and carried Easter lilies. Nurse! Nurse!"

"It's all right, Minnie."

They tried to comfort each other.

 *Five*

Booble-de-boo-boo-boo. Boo-ble-de-boo-boo-boo.

In the warm shower, Arthur lathered his skinny chest, slapping it in time to a tune that had stuck in his mind from the institution. At the state school you were known for some personal or peculiar trait very quickly—often before people knew your name. Like Gembie. He was a big stormy kid with a loose mouth. Booble-de-boo-boo-boo, he sang all day. He sang it in the chapel under his breath. He yelled it in the shower. He tapped it out in the dining room with spoons. At first they thought it was funny and called him Boo-boo. Then he got on everybody's nerves and there were several fights about it. Finally everybody forgot about it.

Booble-de-boo-boo-boo became like the mush for breakfast
—like the jeans on the wash line.

Arthur had not thought of Gembie in years. But he could
smell him as though he had just passed by. He smelled like
unsatisfied sex. They all did, for that matter. And dirty
feet—but mealy dirt, not black dirt that would wash away.
And Lysol. Those smells had gotten behind his eyeballs and
stayed for many years.

He and Gembie were assigned together to the vegetable
fields. There corn grew, and string beans, tomatoes and mel-
ons. Potatoes and onions were in another field. Their job was
to hoe the weeds, direct the streams of irrigation water, and
pick off the tomato worms. Picking off the worms was
cheaper than spraying them, and this job delighted Gembie.
He would collect the worms in his hat until the hat bulged
with the big furry things, and then with one jump he would
smash them under his foot, delighting in the sound and the
spray of their pus-colored guts.

At first Arthur thought Gembie might be his friend.
After all, they slept in the same room and they had the same
work assignment. But Arthur learned that friendship there
was rare.

"Who needs you?" Gembie would say if Arthur suggested they go to the village together. And once, when Arthur offered to share his piece of pineapple upside-down
cake with him, Gembie had shouted: "What are you, some
dumb fairy?" The other boys had laughed and minced past
Arthur when they left the dining room. "Poop-poop-a-
doop," one of them said.

On visitors' day they dressed up and waited in rows in the
day room.

Visiting hours were from three to five. By three-thirty, if

no one came, the ones who were left would make loud remarks about the visitors. They would snicker and make fart sounds until the supervisor would herd them back to the dormitories.

Arthur could never understand why he had to dress and sit there if he knew no one was coming.

"You never can tell," the supervisor would say, with a big fake smile that would make Arthur want to tie the supervisor's lips together.

Then one gray February the supervisor told him they had tried to locate his parents but apparently they had moved away. Arthur had known this already. He had seen the running look in his mother's eyes the day she brought him there.

"Now I won't have to dress up on visitors' day any more," Arthur said.

"Of course you will," the supervisor said, bringing his big mouth close to Arthur's. "An aunt or an uncle might come. Or maybe a cousin. You never can tell."

Arthur ran away from the state school finally because he fell in love. The woman's name was Ramona and she was dark and fierce and worked in the kitchen. She could throw a knife across the room and have it stick in the wall between two pans. She had a wide belly and arms as big as a man's. She swore like a man, but her laugh was something else. It was the most intimate sound Arthur had ever heard, and he thought that she laughed that way only for him. That summer he watched her from the yard as she stood by the chopping block, her knife flashing over peppers and onions or cutting the huge beef carcasses into roasts and stews. A young Italian boy worked with her in the kitchen and their voices were never silent.

"Ah, you are a dumb bastard," she would shout at him, whetting the knife and slashing a cabbage into a fine slaw. "Here, put this into your pot!" and she would brush the cabbage into her apron and dump it into the roaring pot on the stove. The boy would shout back in a language Arthur could not understand, but the insinuation of the boy's inflection made Arthur weak with jealousy.

She spotted Arthur in the yard after a few days.

"You!" she beckoned to him with her knife. "You." And then she laughed.

From that day he was permitted in the kitchen. The young Italian boy, who in turn should have been jealous if he had known of Arthur's strong love for Ramona, barely acknowledged his presence outside of occasionally throwing him a lump of sugar butter or a crisp carrot. It was as though Arthur were a dog who didn't count. But Ramona knew about him. She poked him with the tip of her knife, sometimes running it down the part in his hair, laughing at his apprehension. With the back of her hand she wiped his mouth as if it were her own. She cut his fingernails with a pair of vegetable shears. And once in a while she would peer for long minutes into the depths of his ears as if she had lost something there.

"Ah, kiddo," she would say—she never called him anything else—"Ah, kiddo, what you got in there?" And she would beckon to the Italian boy and with serious eyes they would both look.

He fell in love with her like a foolish hound dog falls in love with its master. He mooned, he thrilled, he followed her, he thought about her day and night. He had no discrimination about her—he thought every hair, every lump, every gesture was the most beautiful thing he had ever seen.

At night he would lie in bed and spin story after story about what he would do with her and would end up having to roll over on his hand.

Finally one day he decided to tell her. Too bad, he thought later.

"I've got to tell you something," he said furtively to Ramona when the young Italian boy left the kitchen for a moment.

"Yeah, kiddo. Yeah, yeah." She looked at him sharply out of the corner of her eye. He was panicked now because already things had changed. The knife had stopped in mid-air. She was waiting. He wanted to turn back, to undo the thing before the disaster was completed. Let me be back in the yard looking at her, he thought, before she ever noticed me. There was a buzzing in his ears which shut out all other sounds but his own voice ringing hollow in his head. He could not stop.

"You probably think I'm stupid . . ." (She nodded at him philosophically) . . . "but I go for you, Ramona."

Her eyes moved slowly, taking in all aspects of him. She walked toward him as though she were dancing, her knife hanging by her side. Then as she came close, the knife shot out, slicing off the buttons of his pants in one slashing motion. His pants dropped to the floor, leaving him stunned and quite exposed in front of her. There was a long moment in which neither of them moved. Outside, Arthur could hear the shouts of the youngest boys playing baseball. The sounds were clear but very thin, as if they were coming from miles away. Ramona watched. He was as stunned as though he had been stung by a thousand spiders. Then her lips moved in a whisper as she reached for him. At this moment the young Italian boy returned to the kitchen.

The words she was about to say were replaced by a hoarse cry: "Eh, Umberto, look what we got! A boy who has lost his buttons." Umberto joined her laughter, slapping his sides at the sight of Arthur, whose thin white legs were frozen in immobility.

"Hey, skinny boy," Umberto shouted, pointing to Arthur's nudity, "why you do like that? Ha, Ramona, he look like some dirty old man!" His own joke set him off into spasms of laughter, until he was bent helplessly over the sink. Ramona had gone back to her chopping block. Arthur pulled up his pants, holding them in a bunch in front. What had she been going to say before Umberto interrupted? He looked for a clue in her eyes, but saw only mockery. The sight of Arthur with his pants *up* struck the Italian boy even funnier. He staggered from the sink to Ramona, draping himself over her back as the tears streamed down his face. Arthur turned and ran.

That night, between 11:00 and 11:30, he had a fit in his bed which woke several of the boys in the dormitory. He ran away the next day, his mind thick and syrupy under a heavy dose of Dilantin.

Arthur got a job as a Western Union messenger by telling the man that he had done the same kind of work in Buffalo.

"Is that a fact?" the man said, looking suspiciously from under his green sun visor. "Are you fast on your feet?"

"Yes, sir."

"And how do you talk to women?"

"As little as I can, sir."

The man thought this was a great joke and gave Arthur the job. He did not notice that Arthur was bearing most of

his weight on his right leg because the lef
bling with weakness.

Arthur took a room above the Majestic The
first pay check he bought a bunch of artificial flowers
put them on the dresser. The following week he bought a
sampler, hand-painted in Japan to look like petit point,
which said: *Home is Where the Heart Is*. He thought these
two objects would make the big baggy room more cheerful,
but they did not. In fact, it looked even drearier. When I
have my own house, he thought, I will hang the sampler in a
sunny entryway.

Once in a while he would sit in the lobby, but he felt
uncomfortable there, as though he were a long way from
home. Also the lobby had green linoleum on the floor, which
reminded him of the state school. Most of the time he sat
upstairs on the bed, reading or trying to rest or wondering
what was to become of him. Now and then he thought of
Ramona and what it was she had been about to say to him
before the Italian boy came into the kitchen.

Six

The hospital at night was like a yellow pocket tied to the outside world by a stream of visitors, by raucous blooming azalea plants delivered in green ribbon and foil, and by a petulant little man who came in once a day to sell the newspaper. For the patient who remained hospitalized a long time, an insidious metamorphosis took place—the outside world dimmed and faded like a watercolor exposed to the sun, while the hospital became the center and the only real part of the universe. Doctors and nurses seemed to have been born and raised in the hospital, with only short punctuations of absenteeism for such things as schooling and marriage. During the day it was easier to believe that the staff might go off to their own lives in houses and apartments quite separate from the hospital, but at night the staff surely seemed to emerge from hidden vaults within the walls.

One of the long-term patients for whom the outside world ceased to exist was Minnie. She was dying slowly, cheerfully, and without causing any real trouble. Occasionally she would rally in response to a drug, almost as if to please the young resident or intern who gave it to her. Then she would decline again, and the nurses would sit and talk to her, each of them hoping she would not die on her shift. (Strangely enough, a large number of nurses had never seen a dead person. They could smell the approach of death and always managed to change shifts with someone to whom death did not seem so impertinent.)

Minnie was dying, but she would not die, and this was the only surprise she presented to the staff. At morning report, she was the last patient to be discussed. She's still here, the one crew would say to the next. Still hanging on. Such a good old sport. Giggling in the teeth of death. Giving us a lesson to learn. The whispered sound in her throat was not a giggle or even the death rattle as they imagined (and had, on two occasions, reported as such), but the sound of fear lurking there. The good old sport was scared—scared silly? scared to death? A few of the nurses loved her because she rarely had visitors and because she had such dreadful things wrong with her. The odd juxtaposition of love and horror was not questioned by many.

In moments of deep crisis when death came too close, shutting down a vital organ for too long a time, or when permission for another procedure was needed, a call would go out to Minnie's family and they would come, led by a big strong daughter and followed by several tall men who might be sons or nephews, usually a teenager with a transistor held to his ear, and a young girl who chewed gum and stared at the handsome orderlies.

"Turn off that radio, Lee-roy." And the boy would do what he was told and then make a brave attempt to kiss the dying old woman. The men were sweet and strong and would circle Minnie in their arms as if she were a pretty, young girl. That was the only time Minnie really smiled. At those times her smile was so private that her daughter looked away.

Miss Oxford, the head nurse, loved Minnie because she felt it was part of her charge. Also, she was particularly intrigued with the care and maintenance of the many mechanical devices required to keep Minnie alive. The routine of this care—moving along logical lines from contamination to sterility—was a comfort to Miss Oxford. At these times her pale eyes were especially bright. She hummed a little four-note tune, or spoke softly to herself in Latin phrases. "*Ad hoc*," she might say as she arranged things in the sterilizer. (She often used this phrase as an expectorant to loosen the phlegm in her throat. *Ad hoc!*) But her favorite was "*Sic semper morbidis*," which she had arrived at by modifying the motto of her home state, Virginia: "*Sic semper tyrannis*." She often greeted the patients with this in the morning. (*Sic* indeed, Warren had said.) For troublesome times, such as nights with insomnia or grand rounds with visiting foreign professors, she would occupy herself with abbreviations or with *hic, haec, hoc*, building tunes around them or arranging them in poetic form. Hicity, haecity, hoc, the mouse ran up the clock . . . Yes, Dr. Shaw, q.i.d. Yes, Dr. Shaw, q.i.d. P.r.n. and q.i.d., don't try to make a monkey out of me.

Sometimes Miss Oxford smiled at what went on in her own mind.

When Miss Oxford was satisfied that Warren and Arthur and Junie Moon really intended to live together, she notified the social worker.

"I thought you would like to know," she whispered. "I think it is their unconscious wish to re-create the primal scene."

"Oh my God," said Binnie Farber, the social worker, "you've been attending too many psych conferences." That day after lunch she got Warren aside and asked him about the plan. She liked Warren. His flamboyant resolve in the face of alarming odds touched her. Don Quixote in a wheelchair.

"It was just a thought," he said, his face neutral in the depths of his beard.

"Indeed!" Binnie Farber said.

"Miss Farber, I have known you for seven years and you have yet to believe a thing I say."

"Keep trying," she advised.

"She will help us," Warren said to Arthur. "Farber always plays it cool so I won't know what she's thinking."

"Do you?"

"Of course!" Warren then decided it was time to speak further about Junie Moon. "I've decided," he said, "that we would be foolish to include a woman in our plans."

"What?"

"Junie Moon is a liability."

Arthur thought for a long time before he answered. His hands played nervously over the lapel of his bathrobe, and his head got involved in a sideways spasm which took time to control. So far, Warren had made all the plans. He had a scrapbook and a map of the city and some want-ads circled for various job offerings. He was oppressively controlling.

"I like Junie Moon," Arthur said at last.

"Naturally," Warren said. "But that's not the issue. I like her too. As a matter of fact, I think she's a fine person."

"I see," Arthur said.

"I would imagine that she is of at least average intelligence."

"What's that got to do with it?"

"Of course, I couldn't testify to her moral character."

"No," said Arthur, "you would hardly qualify."

"Now you listen here—"

"You listen for a change." Arthur was growing white with the effort of asserting himself. He hated the physiological changes that accompanied anger or arguing—the cold sweat and the violent tremors particularly. "You've already invited her. What do you propose to do about that?"

"I thought we would both talk to her."

"Both? Do your own dirty work." With that, he walked off in the direction of his bed.

"Don't run away," Warren said, pursuing him in his wheelchair. "I'm talking to you."

"That's what I'm trying to avoid."

"But if we're to live together, we can't start by developing bad habits. As adults, we must talk things through."

"I'm not sure any more that any of us are going to live together," Arthur said, looking down at his shoe.

Warren paled visibly beneath his beard and looked as

though Arthur had threatened his life. When he spoke, the malice had gone from his voice and he sounded childish and uncertain.

"All right, you can have Junie Moon," he said, as if she were a marble or a baseball glove he was trading. "I don't care enough about her to waste my breath."

This was one of the few fights Arthur had ever won in his life, and he thought he was going to cry. And while he was trying to prevent this, he was also trying to remember every excruciating detail of what had just happened—what the formula had been. Who knows, he thought, I might want to win again.

Seven

Grand Rounds, in which a large group of doctors, nurses, medical students, and usually a visiting dignitary or two went from bed to bed to discuss the patient's progress or decline, were held on Wednesday beginning at 9:30 in the morning. At this time, either the young intern or the resident stood stiffly at the foot of the patient's bed and recited the story of the illness. He was careful to put all the fact to memory, knowing that some of his Attendings were more interested in phosphate levels, and some more apt to quiz him about renal function.

Preparations for the rounds began the night before when a porter came to mop the floors, often between the hours of midnight and one, banging his bucket against the beds as he moved the hampers and nightstands. He was followed by a waxing-machine man at about 3 A.M. Ed, the mopper, was a dour and sour smelling man whose heavy mop moved like a fat snake across the floor. He regarded the patients as if they were serving time for some grave crime they had committed. Vernon, the waxer, moved his machine as if he were in a dream. Sometimes a thin moaning came from his lips which might have been singing.

At five instead of six on the morning of Grand Rounds, the night staff switched on the lights and made their own rounds with pans, pills, and thermometers. The patients were told to scrub and brush and get into white hospital gowns. Flowers and other personal objects were hidden away and replaced by sterile trays for bandaging or probing.

"Help!" Warren said to Miss Holt. "You are scrubbing the last of me away!"

"But your essence will remain," Miss Holt said. "And if you have any influence over Arthur, ask him not to correct the resident when he presents the lab data. This one tends to hold a grudge."

They came like a flock of white birds and hovered around the first bed on the ward.

"How are you feeling?" A tall, older man always began this way after the resident had recited the facts.

"I feel better, doctor."

"That's good."

"There's only one thing, doctor."

"Yes?" But the doctor had turned to the resident. "By the way, the Schilling test showed what?"

"It's my breathing . . ."

"Of course." But to the resident: "Perhaps you felt the test wasn't necessary?"

"It hurts when I breathe, doctor."

"And a twenty-four-hour urine while you're at it. Now then, how are you feeling?"

"I feel better."

"Good."

"It's my breathing."

"By the way, when you get that urine back, give me a ring in the lab. We've got a young fellow there who might give you a hand." They moved on, discussing a recent study in Cleveland.

Arthur could not drive the thought out of his mind that those on rounds were really members of a choir who would at any time burst into song. He had first had this fantasy when he was a little boy and the endless process of diagnosis began. It was often painful for him to keep from laughing when they stopped at his bed, and sometimes he was unable to control himself. These laughing fits had been interpreted variously, but recently as evidence of plaques developing in his brain, causing emotional lability.

Oh promise me that someday you and I, the lady psychiatrist, standing next to the diabetic specialist, sang in her silent soprano. Her mouth formed a perfect *H* and her tone was clear and uncluttered.

Lightly flying o'er the snow with a hey, ha, ha, ha, warbled Miss Oxford in her uncertain alto, her eyes fixed on the surgical trays.

Let every young married man sing to his wife, the Schilling-test doctor led two other baritones in a drinking song.

Arthur felt sick. His silent shrieks were already swelling in his abdomen, pressing his bladder to dangerous proportions. And he had forgotten to urinate.

"Are you feeling any better?"

He knew they didn't care too much if he answered, but perversely, when he did not, they asked again.

"Yes," his voice was strained, barely audible. Please, please go away, he thought.

"Are you feeling more, ah, depressed?" the lady psychiatrist said.

Ah God help me, Arthur thought, she *was* a soprano, vibrato and all.

The counter-tenor, a sandy little man with neat fingernails, began to test Arthur's reflexes. *And a partridge in a pear tree.* He tapped the patellar tendon. *Four talking birds, three French hens, two turtledoves*—he ran his hammer handle up the sole of Arthur's foot.

"Waaaaaaa!" Arthur shrieked.

The doctor jumped back. "Did I hurt you?" he asked in a high, girlish voice. He was petulant, knowing full well he had not hurt Arthur.

"No," Arthur managed to say. "It's just that . . ."

But the group had turned to go. "Plaques," he heard one of them say.

At Warren's bed, the matter of the living arrangements was brought up.

"Warren and Arthur are planning to share an apartment when they leave the hospital," the resident said, his mouth fixed in a tolerant smile.

"Is that so?" the diabetic doctor said. He winked at Miss Oxford, who looked quickly at the linoleum.

"That is so," Warren said. "Arthur and I and Junie Moon."

"Who?" the doctor said, sensing a joke.

"Junie Moon," the resident said. "The patient with the acid burns."

"Oh, Lord." The doctor had not meant to say "Oh, Lord" and tried to hide his having said it by saying "I see."

"There have been worse plans made in this world," Warren said, looking the doctor straight in the eye.

A young medical student with a baby-face and blond eyelashes snickered and tried to pretend he was clearing his throat.

"What's so damned funny?" Warren said.

The diabetic doctor, now off the hook himself, turned on the medical student. "Yes, Martinson, tell us what's so funny."

Suddenly Martinson's world was spinning. He had not meant to make fun of Warren. He most certainly had not meant to snicker during Grand Rounds and especially in the presence of the diabetic doctor, whom he respected and whom he wanted to think favorably of him.

"Nothing, sir," he said.

The doctor was about to continue his attack, but Warren interrupted.

"We'll invite you to dinner, sometime, doctor," he said cheerfully. "Would you come?"

"Sure," the doctor said with a smile. "I'd love to."

"That's a promise," Warren said, narrowing his eyes.

As they moved on, Martinson, the medical student, hung back.

"I'm sorry," he said to Warren, his eyes as candid as an eight-year-old's. "It's just that it seemed funny to me at the time."

Warren looked at him. "So keep it to yourself," he said.

"I *said* I was sorry," Martinson said, getting a bit peeved.

"I'm unimpressed with your forthrightness . . . and your terrible manners," Warren said.

"Well, I'll be damned," Martinson said, a flush rising to his cheeks.

"And your incredulity," Warren added.

"You'd better watch your own tongue," Martinson said. "Remember you're a patient here."

"Your big baby-face scares me to death!" Warren said. He hopped out of bed like an acrobat and wheeled off in his chair, nicking the medical student's toe as he went by.

Side by side, Junie Moon and Minnie watched the doctors make their rounds. Minnie was always frightened by them, and Junie Moon did her best to reassure her.

"They're going to kill me today," Minnie said softly.

"Of course they won't kill you," said Junie Moon.

"They are going to say 'Minnie, you need another procedure.' And that will be that. How come I need so many procedures?"

"Because you're mean and evil."

Minnie tried to laugh at Junie Moon's joke, but her throat was sore and dry. "This time I won't give permission. I won't do it."

"You've got a right to refuse," Junie Moon said. "After all, that body doesn't belong to anyone but you."

"I know. Poor old thing." She had begun to cry and this made Junie Moon nervous.

"I'll tell you what, when they come by, you tell them first before they can say anything. You speak right up and say 'I don't want any more procedures.' Just say it fast, before they get their minds made up."

"They don't listen to me. They ask me questions, but when I start to answer, they talk to each other."

"You got to talk loud."

"I did once, but that made them mad."

"Well, how about talking to them in French?"

"I don't know how to talk French."

"Maybe they don't either. Then you'd be safe."

"But if they didn't understand, what good would it do?"

"You say they don't listen, so it wouldn't make any difference if you talked French or not."

"You get me all mixed up, Junie Moon."

"Well," Junie Moon said, "at least it takes your mind off yourself."

"Just think, it all started with a little pimple on my finger."

"You're kidding," Junie Moon said, looking at Minnie's tubes and drains. Minnie always blamed that little pimple for her troubles.

"I went to see Doctor Hogg. He lived over the drugstore and had his office in the front parlor. I knew Doctor Hogg for years. He used to take care of my daddy and my mama and all of us, both singly as we came along, and together, like the time we got the mumps. There were seven of us, and the time we had the mumps he went through our house from bed to bed, and some of us was two in a bed, and he looked down our throats and took our fever—even Mama and Daddy was sick. It was like he was making his own Grand Rounds, you know. Only when he asked us how we was feeling, he sat there until we told him. Anyway, a year ago I showed him this pimple and he said Minnie there's nothing wrong with that finger that won't take care of itself . . . just quit worrying about it. So I went home, but I didn't quit worrying about it. Later that week I went to a new doctor. Lord God in the morning, what a mistake that was. If I had only one thing in my life I could do over, it would be to take Doctor Hogg's advice and leave that pimple alone. But oh no, not Minnie. Junie Moon, would you believe that I used to be a big strong woman? Junie Moon, do you know that I'm only fifty-two years old?"

It was the pain, Junie Moon thought. And death being so close all the time. It drained the sap out of bones and left skin hanging loose. It turned hair dry and old. And fingers became claws, as if hanging on were the greatest need.

"You don't look a day over thirty-nine," Junie Moon said.

"Sure. Me and Jack Benny," Minnie said. "But I don't mind your lying. If I look old, tell me a lie. If I'm going to die, tell me another."

"You're not going to die, Minnie."

Minnie was beginning to drift off, as she often did. The talking seemed to have exhausted her. She turned on her side and her voice was barely audible from under the blankets.

"Aunt Tulie brought us green applesauce the time when we were all so sick with the mumps. She brought it in a big flowered bowl and walked from one end of the house to the other with it before she set it down in the kitchen."

There was a long silence, then a giggle, like a child's.

"You know how new-cooked green applesauce smells? It smells fresh. And warm. But if you've got mumps real bad, fresh green applesauce smells only one way: sour! Lord God, Junie Moon, she almost killed us before she set that applesauce down in the kitchen and shut the door! Aunt

Tulie, we yelled at her, take that damn applesauce out of here before you kill us all! You're killing our mump glands with that terrible sour smell! Poor old thing, her feelings was hurt that day all right . . . Aunt Tulie! It's all right, Aunt Tulie."

Then Minnie turned herself slowly in the bed until she was facing Junie Moon. Her expression was like very sick people sometimes get: so uncritical, so unjudgmental that she looked strange and detached.

"I got to ask you a question," she said.

Junie Moon felt something was coming that she did not want to be asked. She had a way of sensing things like that, like an old dog examining the wind with his nose.

"What do you want to ask me," she said after a while.

"When I get better, can I come and live with you and Arthur and Warren?" Minnie said.

"Sure," Junie Moon said. She said it very quickly so that Minnie wouldn't think she was stalling or that she had any doubts about it. After all, if you're going to lie, you might as well do it good and quick.

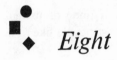 *Eight*

"We have to make some plans," Warren said. "They are beginning not to believe us."

"Your need for approval represents a serious personality defect," Junie Moon replied, peering at him over a copy of *The Resident Physician*.

"Where did you learn that high-falutin' language?" Warren said.

"From Miss Oxford. She attends too many psych conferences and always has a few phrases to spare."

"Nonetheless," he said, "we are becoming known as the whistlers and dreamers. Do you think Arthur really wants to live with us?"

Junie Moon put the magazine down slowly and stared at him. "Your need to set one person fighting with another is also a serious personality defect. That is my own conclusion. Maybe it's *you* who doesn't want to live with *us*."

"Ridiculous."

"First it was me you wanted to get rid of. Don't deny it. Now it's Arthur."

"I just wanted everybody to be sure."

"Of what?"

"That they . . . oh hell, I don't know. You're such a nag."

"Somebody has to nag you. I've noticed that on many occasions you are prone to take the bit in your teeth if the other person happens to be shy."

"It would be a sorry state if none of us had leadership qualities," he said. "Besides, most people like to be told what to do."

"That theory is advanced by people who tell people what to do. But since you worry so much about who's going to be boss, why don't you go ahead and take the reins. I, for one, will nominate you and vote for you. We'll ask Arthur. If it's okay with him, it's okay with me." She ducked back into her magazine as if the matter were settled.

"Now you're putting me on," he said.

"Not at all. I believe in setting a person's mind at rest if it is humanly possible."

"Please put that magazine down and talk to me. Why do you read it anyway?"

"I like to see what job opportunities are available."

"But why? You're not a doctor."

"Jesus, Warren, I know that." She gave him a hard look with her damaged eye. "What kind of plans do we need to make?"

"I made a list," he said, taking it out of his bathrobe. "I'll read it to you and see what you think."

"No, please," she said. "I can't concentrate when people read out loud. I get too busy listening to the sound of their voices and watching their tongue." She took the list from him and looked at it for a moment in perplexed silence.

"Warren, I don't understand what this list is all about. It says here: potatoes, garbage, taking turns, banking . . . What does it all mean?"

"I recorded things as I thought of them. There's nothing there that doesn't need consideration."

"Well, while you're at it, you'd better put down 'get apartment.'"

"I thought we might find a house," he said after a while. "When I lived in Boston, we had a house, and I will never forget it."

"Who would clean it?" she said.

"In Boston a woman came twice a week and things were as neat as a pin when she left."

Junie Moon went back to her magazine.

"There was a lovely smell of furniture polish," he said, and he was caught by a sudden stab of longing for his grandmother and Guiles.

"As our leader, you are certainly impractical," Junie Moon said. "Where in hell is this cleaning woman coming from? And what is she to be paid with?" She saw the flicker of pain on Warren's face. At least she thought it was pain—he with his beard, Arthur with his tics and fits, she with her scars and stitches—it was hard for any of them to tell what the other was feeling. But she tried to let him know.

"Warren, I think your idea of a house is fine. Very fine.

Maybe that social-worker lady of yours could help us find one."

Warren smiled. "We could take turns with the cleaning," he said.

They watched Arthur approach from down the corridor. If anything, his gait was worse. It began with an abrupt lurch which set off a series of burpie little steps, each one less predictable than the last. These little steps would finally peter out, like a stone skipping over the water, and then the sequence would begin again, with the lurch hurling him into motion. All the while, his hands flew from side to side and from top to bottom, futilely trying to keep the balance. If one observed closely, there was a predictable rhythm to his walk, a kind of seven-beat cadence reminiscent of a dissonant passage of electronic music. As Warren watched, he thought that Guiles would have composed a little tune for Arthur to walk by. Then he realized that, as time passed, he was attributing more of his own wicked thoughts to Guiles.

"Lordy, lordy," Junie Moon said.

"We'd better not have any scatter rugs in our house," Warren replied.

"It's not going to work," Arthur said after one huge spasm of effort and control landed him in a chair.

"Mr. Gloom has descended," Junie Moon said.

"I'm just being practical," he said. "Where is the money coming from?"

"We'll find a way," Warren said. "The main thing is to find a house."

"It's not the main thing. The main thing is money," Arthur said.

"Maybe I could find a job," Junie Moon said.

Warren quickly looked down at his thin, atrophied legs and busied himself with his brace. Arthur tried to speak, but the words were jammed by a contraction in his throat which shook the muscles of his shoulders and back. Junie Moon glanced slowly from one to the other. They were going to have to talk about each other some day, she thought.

At last the words escaped Arthur's throat. "You wouldn't have to do that," he said. "I could try to get my messenger's job back."

"I look pretty terrible, eh?" Junie Moon said.

"No," Arthur said. "It's getting better every day."

"You're just getting used to me." She turned her head away.

"Please don't do that," Warren said. "I never know what to do when women feel bad."

"What do you do when men feel bad?" Arthur said.

"Guiles used to cry now and then, as I remember. And I would rub the back of his neck. This seemed to have a soothing effect on him. After a while he would shake himself like a dog and then he would be over it. But, with women, if you say anything they cry all the louder."

"I only saw my mother cry once," Arthur said. "She was sitting on the back steps of our house when I came home from school and her face was red and twisted. She never would tell me about it."

"Anyway," Warren said, "the emphasis on women being beautiful is all out of proportion."

"Ugly women have to listen to that statement all their

lives," Junie Moon said. "So kindly shut up. I was always ugly, but now, Jesus . . ." Her voice trailed off.

"You don't have to work right away," Arthur said. "There's no terrible hurry."

"We'll go on relief, like everyone else," Warren said.

"The hell we will," Arthur shouted. His voice was so loud that Ed, who was mopping the floor at the end of the corridor, looked up and cocked his head to one side.

"Oh, Lord," Warren said, "we've now got to contend with your feelings about charity."

"You're damned right. No fat, self-righteous investigator is going to come barging into *my* house," Arthur said.

"Ah, so you object to the investigator, not the principle. Good. I'll ask them to send a pretty, skinny, un-self-righteous one."

"Nobody!" With this, Arthur leaped to his feet, shattering an ashtray as he went. The memory of charity sheets, charity underwear, charity food swept his mind. He remembered the man in the office of the state school trying to detain his mother long enough to get her to fill in the form: Any savings or other assets, madam? Bonds? Any insurance, pensions, annuities, or dividends? I must ask the questions. Of course, the boy is entitled to care. *I am entitled to care in a school for the feeble-minded,* Arthur thought. A short laugh exploded from his lips.

"I don't hear *you* talking about a job," he said to Warren.

"You know that's out of the question," Warren said, slightly elevating his chin as if to dispose of the subject.

"I do not know that," Arthur persisted.

"I have a serious urinary problem," Warren said, "in addition to my paraplegia."

"Balls," Arthur said.

"Not exactly," Warren said.

"We've got to take the welfare," Junie Moon said, "until we get settled and decide what to do." To Arthur she said: "Don't worry so much about it."

"That's what I told him," Warren said.

"Keep quiet," she said, "you are both boring me to death. You remind me of my two maiden aunts. One of them was short and sweet. The other was tall and sad. Rarely an hour passed that they didn't argue about something. They had lived together for so many years that they mistook their arguments for conversations. It was yes-no and no-yes all the time. If one of them had to leave for any length of time —to go to the store, for example—the other would continue the argument, taking both parts, until the one who had gone returned and was able to fend for herself. It was their whole life. I don't think they ever heard a word another person said."

"I had two aunts too," Arthur said. "They would sit on the couch and swing their feet together all evening long without saying a word. They worked in the bank, side by side."

"I didn't have any aunts at all," Warren said. "Now what do you think of that?"

"You could have mine," Arther said.

"I had fourteen altogether," Junie Moon said. "None of them were at all distinguished."

"I had none," Warren said.

"I had an uncle who teased them," Arthur said. He flushed as if he were telling something frightfully personal. " 'Well now,' he would say to them, talking as if they were one person instead of two. 'How is your love life?' He would always start up with them in that way, and they would giggle and hang their heads. And he would say something like 'How about the butcher, I hear *he's* looking for a wife,' and this would set them to giggling even louder. 'I saw him making eyes at both of you last Saturday,' he would shout and they would shriek and slap each other on the back as if that was the funniest thing they had ever heard in their lives." Arthur took a deep breath. He rarely talked so much.

"They probably didn't know what else to do," Junie Moon said.

"They sound moronic to me," Warren said.

"Didn't I tell you?" Arthur said. "Morons run in my family." He sat down and faced the wall.

"Oh damn," said Junie Moon. "We've hurt his feelings." She put her arm around his thin shoulders and patted him with her torn, disfigured hand. "Look, Arthur, we've all got something wrong. You and me and Warren and Minnie. The doctors and Miss Oxford . . . Do you know that Miss Oxford has never slept with anybody in her whole life? When you've got that wrong with you, you're in trouble."

"How do you know about Miss Oxford?" Warren asked testily.

"It's common knowledge," Junie Moon said.

"That's a terrible thing to say," Warren said, slamming his hand on the arm of his wheelchair.

"How come you're getting so upset?" Arthur said.

"What a person does in their own bed is their own business," Warren said. He disliked the subject because he was afraid they would discover that he was a virgin.

"Miss Oxford would be flattered to know that she had such a champion," Junie Moon said.

"Please shut up," Warren said.

"On the other hand," Junie Moon went on, "it might make her nervous."

"Why should it make her nervous?" asked Arthur, who loved to talk about sex. He moved closer to Junie Moon, who still had her arm around his shoulder.

"Because people like to keep their little secrets to themselves. It's like growing mushrooms in the cellar and running down to take a look at them now and then."

"I don't think she'd be very good in bed," Arthur said, trying to sound casual and experienced.

"You never can tell," said Junie Moon. "Sometimes you turn a virgin loose, and wow! Hang on to your hat."

"You can say that again!" Arthur said, smiling directly at Junie Moon.

"Baloney," said Warren, turning down the corners of his mouth.

"I met one while I was at the state school," Arthur said. He was lying, but he was very pleased at how easily he did it. He hoped Junie Moon would not remove her hand. "She was the daughter of the livestock superintendent," he continued, "and she was so afraid she was going to be raped by one of the feeble-minded boys that she never came out of the house." He leaned back, feeling more at ease than he had in years. The terrible tensions of his body were gone. "Well, one day I was out in the tomato patch with a crazy idiot named Gembie who collected worms in his hat, and I saw her come out on the porch. She had just washed her hair and was about to dry it in the sun."

"Hell," Warren said, "how did you know that?"

"There are certain things a man knows," he said, looking down his nose at Warren. Junie Moon gave him a big grin. "She had great big legs and wore a short skirt and when she sat down in that rocking chair on the porch, man, I could see to the North Pole."

"I don't blame her for being scared with boys leering at her out of the tomato patch," Junie Moon said.

"I didn't leer at her. I walked right up to the porch and said 'Hi.' It was as simple as that."

"*What* was as simple as that?" Warren said.

Arthur hesitated for a split second, but Warren noticed.

"Why, getting her to do what I wanted," Arthur said.

"You're a damned liar!" Warren said gleefully. "You're making up the whole thing!" He had caught Arthur out.

"I am not!" Arthur said petulantly, but he looked gloomy and uneasy.

"It sounded pretty authentic to me," Junie Moon said. "I mean about the boy collecting the worms and all."

"It doesn't to me," Warren said. "And anyway, we're supposed to be making our plans, instead of sitting around telling dirty stories."

"Now you're sounding like Miss Oxford, who never got laid," Arthur said. "I hope you're not setting out to be our housemother."

"Warren said *he* would like to be the boss," Junie Moon said. "As a matter of fact, I said it was all right with me."

"It is not all right with me," Arthur said.

"There are certain advantages in letting him be boss," Junie Moon said. "You ought to think about them before you make a final decision."

"Name one," Arthur said.

"Like paying the rent," Junie Moon said. "If the landlord gets used to him paying the rent every month, you and I wouldn't get hounded for it. See?"

"Yeah, I see. But most of the time it works out bad. Like

at the state school. We'd elect a guy and in ten minutes he'd turn mean. There's something about being elected that brings out the rotten, even in a good guy. If Warren wants to be boss, then let him try without our having to say so."

"But that's no fun," Warren said.

Arthur laughed. "You see what I mean? If he can't be elected and rotten, he doesn't want to play."

The three of them were talking in a corridor that was long and gray and opened into what was called the sun room. The windows in the sun room were pasted shut summer and winter and there was always a sweet sick smell of cigarette smoke and wax. There were five chairs with green plastic covers which were worn through on the arms, and a green plastic couch in front of a television set. A vase of faded plastic roses was on the TV and that was the only decoration. In the evenings, those patients who were able would take their visitors to the sun room. Some of them would laugh and talk, making it hard to hear the programs. Other visitors would sit staring at the set, scarcely exchanging a word with the sick person they had come to see. Once in a while a young husband would pull one of the chairs to the side and speak softly to his sick wife, patting her from time to time as though this would make the reason for his fears go away.

Warren and Junie Moon and Arthur seldom went to the sun room in the evening because no one ever visited them and because they found the TV programs fragmented and dull. Instead, they gathered in the corridor and made it more home-like by bringing with them a small stool which they used as a table and on which they placed an ashtray and little decorations such as a flower or a bright colored ad from a magazine. This was Warren's idea, who insisted that morale was maintained by such efforts. Most of the time the ad was for some kind of lavishly prepared food such as angel cake stuffed with strawberries and topped with candy sprinkles, or a barbecue buffet served in the spacious patio of Mrs. So-and-so's California home. "Gracious living," Warren would say, propping up the ad, "does not require a lavish budget."

"Ho!" was usually Junie Moon's reply.

As they talked about whether Warren would be boss, their voices took on the kind of singsong phrasing of old friends who have spent long hours together. Once in a while Arthur would unintentionally interrupt the rhythm with a spasm, but aside from this and Warren's high, tentative laugh, their voices droned like bees on a hot summer after-noon. The other patients observed this with various reac-tions. To Minnie, who could hear but not see them, their voices were a comfort. It reminded her of her childhood in the country when she would be sent indoors to bed while the grownups sat talking in the yard until the sky drew dark and the stars came out. Young John Goren, who had lost his leg and who could no more tolerate deformity in himself than in those around him, was pointed in his disapproval. "Oh Jesus," he would say in a loud sigh as he hobbled past on his crutches, "you three again!" They ignored him, although at times Warren had a deep craving to trip him or to say something mean.

Miss Holt, the assistant nurse, often joined them as though she had been invited, like a fourth for bridge. "Well," she would say cheerily, "what the hell are you up to?"

"You shouldn't talk that way," Warren would say, shak-ing his finger at her, "or you will be strung up and fried by the mother superior."

Miss Holt liked them, that was true, and they laughed and

joked together, but without even knowing it they waited for her to leave.

"Junie Moon," Minnie would call. "Is that you out there?"

"Yes, Minnie, it's me."

"I hear you talking. You and Warren and Arthur are talking half the night away."

"That's right, Minnie."

"Sitting around your little table, talking and talking."

"She wants to come and live with us," Junie Moon whispered to Warren and Arthur.

"Well, she can't!" Warren said. "We have enough trouble as it is."

"Keep your voice down," Junie Moon said. "I didn't tell her she could."

"What's wrong with her family? Why can't they take her?" Warren's voice was rising and his face was getting red under his beard.

"Shut up," Arthur hissed at him.

"It would take all three of us to look after her," Warren said.

John Goren hobbled past. "Oh Jesus," he groaned. "Don't you three ever get tired of each other?"

"Lord yes," Junie Moon said. "Why don't you come and sit down?" Goren was so surprised he stopped and leaned against the wall. Junie Moon offered him part of a Hershey bar she took from her bathrobe pocket. Goren did not want to take it because there were fingers missing from the hand that held it to him, but he did despite himself, feeling pale and shaky.

"My girlfriend is supposed to come tonight," he said. "She's late."

"How come she hasn't been here before?" Warren asked.

"She works at night. Telephone operator."

"Yeah? Well, good luck," Warren said.

"What do you mean by that?" Goren said.

"Nothing."

"She would have gotten docked a night's pay if she had come."

"Sure."

"Hell, my mother told her about my leg. It wasn't that."

"Some women wouldn't mind," said Junie Moon.

"Right! And my girl is one of them."

"Some girls would actually prefer a man with a leg missing," Junie Moon said.

"Yeah?" Goren said.

"I hear there are girls who like men better if they got a humpback or if they're dwarfs."

Goren was indignant. "My girl is no damned pervert, if that's what you mean."

"Of course not," she said. "She probably is a pretty little thing and worried to death about you."

"Then why didn't she come to see him before now?" Warren said.

"She's afraid of hospitals, I think," Goren said. "She said once they made her nervous."

"They make me nervous too," Arthur said, laughing, and as if to emphasize his point, his body was rocked with a tremor.

"That's a lot of crap, being afraid of hospitals," Warren said. "People say that when they don't want to come and see you. I know."

"I've got to admit I never liked to visit people in the hospital," Junie Moon said. "I was always afraid they'd die while I was there. And the smells used to bother me—the ether. I knew I would faint and that would be the end of me. Lordy, lordy, I was a sissy in those days."

"I went to visit my cousin once," Arthur said. "I'd never seen her in a nightgown before, and not only that, but when she rolled over in the bed, I saw her big white behind. It was terrible."

Goren looked at his watch. "She probably missed the bus," he said.

"My two maiden aunts got sick together," Junie Moon said. "Whatever one got, the other got, and in this case I think it was gallstones. Well, I knew if I went to visit them, *both* of them would die on me. I yelled and screamed and said I wouldn't go, but my daddy dragged me there and threatened to take out my tonsils if I didn't stop yelling. My folks never thought that kids had problems. Either a kid did what you said or he didn't, and if he didn't, you beat the hell out of him until he did."

"Did they die?" Arthur said. He always moved close to Junie Moon when she was telling a story and now his face was less than a foot away. Junie Moon didn't mind particularly, but she pushed him back without even thinking, much as you would swipe at a pesky gnat.

"Of course they didn't die," she said. "They just sat there in their beds moaning and groaning in tune, and all the louder when visitors came. Do you know that they had the same fever and the same heartbeat and the same blood pressure? Why the Lord took the trouble to create two of them when one would do was beyond me."

When Goren first caught sight of his girl in the corridor, he did not believe it was she. There had been so many long days and nights without her, he had lost track of the details of her face and the sound of her voice. She had sent him notes and candy and once a pair of plaid slippers. Two slippers—she probably hadn't even thought. And she talked to him on the phone, but it was her telephone operator's voice —cheerful and bright and like a telephone-company recording. "Hello, Johnnie, it's Marilyn. I'm fine, and how are *you?*" Everything sounded fake. "Your mother says you're a lot better. I'm sure going to try to come real soon, hon. Real soon."

He turned to run. He would have to see her another day —another time when he felt up to it. She would have to understand that. But his leg was missing and he was not about to run anywhere. Instead he sat down and crossed his good leg over his stump and looked wildly for a blanket with which to hide himself.

The girl saw him and waved, but her hand stopped in mid-air as if she too had had a second thought. Then she turned very pale and walked quickly toward him, kissed him on the lips, avoided looking at the missing leg. She was armed with books and games and candy and she gave them all to Goren at once, looking as though she were sorry she hadn't brought more. She stood on one foot and then the other, afraid to sit down, not knowing what to do with her own whole body, her forehead growing more pale and moist and her hands moving across her face and the front of her blouse as if she were trying to catch on to something firm.

"How have you been?"

"Just fine," Goren said.

"I'm glad to hear that," she said in a rush. "I was worried to death."

She saw the sour look of disbelief come over his face, and

her stomach turned once and she was afraid she was going to vomit.

"I saw Ellen the other day. She said to tell you hello."

"She came to see me here a couple of times."

"I know it," the girl said. They tried to look at each other but their eyes wouldn't hold. "How is the food?"

Goren looked at her hand, which was level with his eyes, and thought: Why can you talk to strangers, and not to your girl? "The food," he said, "is like distilled garbage." This jolted her, but she still could not look at him.

"I made you some cookies," she said. "They are in that green box."

He thought: If I don't say it now, I never will.

"They chopped off my leg," he said.

She swayed as though she had been belted by a prize fighter.

"Take my chair," Arthur said. The girl looked at the others for the first time. She tried to smile at Arthur, but then she saw Junie Moon.

"Oh dear," she said in a voice that was full of pain and horror. And instinctively she moved close to Goren as if for protection. Goren saw this and the terrible doubt within him snapped and he took her hand.

"This is Junie Moon," he said gently. "She is really a secret agent sent here to investigate the X-ray technician."

"Ho!" shouted Junie Moon.

"And she has made a number of lewd discoveries," Warren said.

The girl giggled.

"Most of them concerning everyone except the X-ray technician," Arthur said.

The girl pulled the chair close to Goren and rested her hand on his shoulder.

"There are many things about hospital life which are quite unbelievable," Warren said, smiling at the girl.

"For example," said Junie Moon, "did you know that the hospital is haunted with ghosts who suffer from phantom pains?"

"Phantom pains?" the girl said.

"Yes," Goren said. "That is a terrible ache for something that was dear to you and that went away."

The girl put her arms around Goren and began to weep.

◆ *Nine*

It was a hot Wednesday afternoon when Warren and Arthur and Junie Moon left the hospital. It took some persuading to get discharged at the same time, but Warren arranged it with the resident, promising to send him a bottle of Scotch the following day. "After all," Warren said, "we are about as rehabilitated as we will ever be," and the resident had to agree to that. Before they left, the doctors went over their charts and made their final notes and observations. They felt that they had done all they could for Junie Moon for the time being and that Warren was probably better than he had been in years, but it was Arthur who perplexed and defeated them. The doctors did not like to state publicly in the chart that they had no idea whatsoever what Aruthur was suffering from, so as a consequence they wrote long and sometimes witty statements about the various probabilities. The wit was designed to take the reader's mind off the uncertainties at hand. A large group of those who had seen Arthur through the years were inclined to think that his problems were psychological. They said that Arthur was angry because he had not received the love that was due him, and that he could only express this anger by having a fit. His smaller tremors apparently were expressions of lesser annoyances. The neurologists, however, were more apt to disagree with this theory, feeling that the brain had not yet revealed its complexities.

One of the few doctors whom Arthur liked was a small round man named Fielding who had seen him years ago. Fielding claimed that most neurological difficulties were a matter of faulty wiring or plumbing and that eventually man should have his brain and central nervous system stamped out on a cardboard circuit like a radio set and then there would be fewer causes for breakdown. He had looked carefully into Arthur's eyes and the other tunnels to his brain as if he might find the answer there. Once he had put his own ear to Arthur's head, but he told Arthur that all he heard was a tiny brass band playing *The Stars and Stripes Forever*. Finally Fielding sat down with a sigh next to Arthur's bed and said: "Boy, I have no idea in this world what is causing your ailment and I don't even know where it will take you." And then he talked for more than an hour about himself and how he had become a neurosurgeon because he was driven by a terrible curiosity, and what he had felt when he had seen his first living brain, and how he longed to know more of the mysteries of the universe which lay

locked there. Arthur had felt the man's purpose in life, and
even though he couldn't apply it to himself, somehow he
felt better.

Arthur tried for the most part not to think of his difficulty because if he did he found himself on a bleak and silent
road. The seizures were not so bad. He knew they would
pass as they had come, and to a certain degree he had learned
to protect himself from his own flailing, if not from the em-
barrassment of the attacks. But the weakness was another
matter. It was as if one side of himself were turning to lard
—as if the bones and muscle were melting and only the
weight of them remained. Eventually he knew it would in-
vade his chest and throat and he would strangle on his own
secretions. Although Arthur had not been told this, he
sometimes would imagine that his throat was contracting or
that the walls of his chest were being caved in by an enormous weight. Then the dream about it began and recurred
with dreadful punctuality—a dream of drowning in a pool
of mucus-thick substance, while the doctors watched from
the sidelines, their chins in their hands. He would awake
sweating and trembling and he found that the only way he
could calm himself was to involve his mind in a most elaborate and complicated act such as making a chess game in his
head and remembering all the moves, or attempting an astro-
nomical arithmetic problem without a pencil. It never occurred to him to talk to anyone at such a time, partly because he had been alone so much of his life and also because
he was afraid that if he spoke of the fear the fact would then
emerge and he would not survive the next night's dream.

The resident cornered him before he left, to "discuss his
situation," and Arthur shook with pity for them both. The

resident had thin, very clean lips, and his eyes jumped from one thing to another but never looked into Arthur's eyes.

"Now then, Arthur, let's sum up what we've done so far," the resident said.

Arthur did not like being called by his first name by the resident because it reminded him of the state school. And he knew that summing up meant a senseless review of facts everybody knew. He guessed the resident would say: "Let's see now, you were in excellent health until you were twelve . . ."

The resident gestured to Arthur to lean back on the pillow. He himself preferred to stride back and forth as he spoke, his starched uniform making a whispering noise as he walked.

"Let's see now," the resident began, "you were in excellent health until you were twelve."

The doctors who treated Junie Moon were friendly and candid because there were no mysteries about her troubles. They had a few regrets, such as they could not supply her with new fingers. "Just can't give you a new hand, Junie Moon," they said, wagging their heads and winking at her. One day she said to them: "Why not?" and they looked at her in genuine surprise. "Why not, little resident?" she said, pleased with her impishness. "Why not call up the hand store and have them send one over?" One of the residents scratched his nose and gave her a long look.

"Because," he said, "the hand store was sold to a tire factory and that's the truth."

Junie Moon loved to be taken down by young boys like

this one with hard eyes and silly smiles, and she poked him in the ribs. "You got a bedside manner that will end you up in jail," she said to him, and they laughed together.

Later on, she confessed a few things to him. He was to have the questionable privilege of being the first and last physician to whom she said anything that mattered to her, and he was so touched by it that he had not mentioned it to anyone for fear he might be asked to discuss it at staff meeting. She told him about the nightmare quality of the maiming—about Jesse and how he had made her take off her clothes and later threw acid on her. But what she had really confessed was her terrible passivity which had permitted the whole thing to happen. "I think I could have stopped it if I had yelled or run or fought or done something. Jesse was a puky little crumb and I must have known he was a weakling; but it was like I was under a spell and could only watch him do all those terrible things to me. Maybe it was because nothing much really had happened to me before that time."

While she said this, the resident had looked at her, and his mouth went slack as he tried to absorb what she was saying. The thing that puzzled the resident about himself was that he understood Jesse's pouring the acid over Junie Moon much better than he understood his making her take her clothes off behind the roadside stand. Then, since this understanding bothered him, the resident began to wonder if he himself might disfigure a woman with acid if properly provoked. One evening he tried to discuss this with his wife, but the look of horror which crept over her face prompted him to put a stop to the entire discussion.

At any rate, the doctors had done what they could for Junie Moon for the time being, meaning that they could no longer stab and pare and rearrange her shattered face and hands. She would have to wait until things calmed down, if they ever would, and then they would see.

"It's like being sentenced," Junie Moon said to the resident she could talk to.

"You're right," he said, putting his hand gently on her face.

"You're a cheery cuss," she said to him, and loped away.

Warren made the arrangements. On Friday he saw an ad in the paper for a house on the edge of town. When Warren phoned, a querulous old woman bickered and snapped as if she had no wish in the world to rent the house to anyone. When she asked Warren about the kind of work he did, he told her he was a mining engineer. He had no intention of saying this, but as he thought it over later, it was perfect. Conservative, a little dusty, and temperate. When the old woman agreed to leave the key in the mailbox, Warren called Binnie Farber and explained his need for money.

"Have you seen the place?" she said.

He dodged the question: "You don't think I'd move into a place I hadn't seen, do you?"

"Yes," she said. "Do you think your grandmother would send you the money?"

"No, no, no, no," Warren screamed and then he began to shed real tears.

"All right," she said, "don't get so upset."

When Warren first met Miss Farber he had been too ashamed to admit that he had no relatives except a mother whom he had never seen, so he told her about his grandmother. He had neglected to add that she had been dead for several years.

"I'm sorry," he said into the phone. Then he went on to tell her about the house, quoting from the sparse ad, but making up the rest. "It's on a quiet street," he said, "and it has a garden and a back yard."

"Why do you need a quiet street?" Binnie Farber asked. But her voice was kindly. Warren knew that she would find them money somewhere.

He told the resident that he and Arthur and Junie Moon would be leaving on Wednesday. He told several other people, including John Goren, whom he invited to dinner with his girlfriend, on Thursday. John had laughed and said maybe they would need a little more time to get settled, but Warren insisted.

"The place is already attractively furnished," Warren said.

The last people he told about the house were Arthur and Junie Moon. They had already heard the news from the other patients and by the time Warren got to them they cut him off dead.

"I have fabulous news," Warren said.

They were playing checkers and it appeared as if neither of them heard him.

"Did you hear what I said?" he asked.

"Your move," Arthur said to Junie Moon.

Junie Moon turned in her chair so that her back was to Warren. She faked a silly, lighthearted gaiety with Arthur, and he returned it. "You're too nice to me, Arthur, letting me get away with this triple jump. But then I knew you were a gentleman right from the beginning. Not like some other people we both know."

"To tell you the truth, Junie Moon," Arthur said, "I didn't see that triple jump at all. You just set it up by your superior playing."

"Why, thank you, Arthur. You are one of the kindest men I have run across in many a day."

"I found us a house," Warren said, pushing between them.

"And you're one of the nicest women I know," Arthur said. "It's obvious this creep would not be a friend of yours. Such a lovely woman couldn't possibly know such a creep as this one."

"Thank you, Arthur, for that compliment. You are certainly correct in your assumption. Your move."

"Damn it to hell, listen to me," Warren said.

"I like checkers better than almost any game," Arthur said. "It's not as simple as it looks."

"That's true," Junie Moon said. "Checkers is a very complicated game. Not like chess, but very complicated if played well."

"Chess makes me nervous," Arthur said. "I think it's because the pieces have names and I feel responsible for their lives."

"We are all being discharged on Wednesday," Warren said, his voice high and indignant.

"I feel so sorry for the bishop," Junie Moon said. "He always seemed apologetic to me."

Arthur laughed. "Yes. And the rook is such a hidebound conservative. What do you think of the horse?"

"I don't know," Junie Moon said. "That piece is so pretty, but the way he moves . . . it's like being in the same room with somebody a whole lot smarter than you."

Arthur flashed a quick smile at her. He was glad that he knew what she meant.

"If you don't talk to me," Warren said, "I'm going to throw this checkerboard into the laundry chute."

They stung him a little longer for his bad manners, and in his effort to make up for this he told a few more lies about the comfort and the ease and the beauty they would encounter when they moved to the house on Wednesday.

"It has a big shade tree and a bed of tulips lining the back fence," Warren said.

"And a porch?" Arthur asked.

"A huge porch!" Warren said without a moment's hesitation.

"I always liked a porch with honeysuckle," Junie Moon said.

"How did you know?" Warren cried.

"Oh, I had a feeling," she said, looking at him sideways as though there were something in what he said that did not quite sit well on her stomach.

"I'm glad we're getting the hell out of here," Arthur said. And for a few seconds the three of them stopped their fencing and smiled at each other like three silly, bright monkeys.

Junie Moon did not know how to tell Minnie that she was leaving the hospital, so she took a deep breath and said, "Minnie, we're going," and Minnie sighed and said, "I know." And then she began to whine and complain and give Junie Moon dirty looks and this made it easier for Junie Moon because heretofore she had thought of Minnie only as brave and one to be pitied.

"Don't think I didn't know," Minnie said, hoisting herself to one elbow and arranging her colostomy tube. "It's the scandal of this hospital."

"Minnie, that doesn't sound like you," Junie Moon said, trying to be kindly and hide her own irritation.

"And may I ask what I'm supposed to sound like?" Minnie snapped.

Junie Moon turned to walk away but Minnie would not let her. "You said I could come and live with you," Minnie said, "but I can see by your sneaky behavior that you never meant it."

"That's not true, Minnie."

"I don't think it was right that you led me to believe that life was going to be a bed of roses when it's going to be a cemetery plot." Junie Moon started to say something, but Minnie silenced her. "To make a promise that you have no intention of keeping is a sin. It's like deciding ahead of time to kill somebody."

Junie Moon sat down. It had been a long time since anybody scolded her and there was a strange comfort in it. Once her father had switched her for lying about something or other and she could feel the same sting now. And she remembered his face—his mouth a stern slit, but an almost twinkle in his eyes. She thought: when men stop enjoying beating on one another, then they will stop beating on one another.

Minnie's skinny little face was bunched up as if she were going to cry.

"I had a mean uncle like you," she said. "He lived in Springfield, Massachusetts, and he drove a little black Ford that he'd owned all his life. Once or twice a year he would come to stay with us and it was like the undertaker coming to call—a little runt of a man as serious as dust and about as interesting. Lord God, his name was James T. Ellsworth. As a matter of fact, you're a lot like James T. Ellsworth, Junie Moon."

"Thanks for the compliment," Junie Moon said.

"The thing I hated about him the very best was that every year when he came to visit he'd promise all us kids he would send us something when he got home. That lying little man would sit us all down on the steps and ask us every time, just before he left, what we wanted him to send. Nothing was too big or too expensive for Uncle James T. Ellsworth to send to his nieces and nephews. Once I ordered a solid-silver tea set and gold-banded dishes to serve eight and he said that would be just fine. That same year my brother Gersh ordered a Rolls-Royce automobile with a Victrola built into the back seat. Uncle James T. Ellsworth said he didn't know where to buy a Rolls-Royce, but he would get Gersh an American La Salle, Victrola and all."

"Well?"

"Well what? That man never sent us those presents. Not those or anything else!"

"Then how come you told him what you wanted, year after year?"

"Because he asked us. Don't you understand anything?"

"Not much," Junie Moon said.

"You also remind me of Miss Mary Lou Elliot, who was my third-grade teacher, who said the person who got the most spelling words would get a prize. I wasn't very good in spelling, but she made that prize sound like it was worth fifty dollars before she was through talking about it. I guess I never studied so much in all my life—neither before or ever again—as I did for that spelling test. I even learned a lot of words I knew she wouldn't ask, just in case she did. Well, I want you to know I won."

"That's very nice," Junie Moon said.

Minnie's face turned red. "That was *not* very nice," she yelled. "It was not nice at all because the prize that she'd been talking about for half the year, bragging and boasting about it as if it came from the Queen of Sheba's palace, turned out to be a stupid goddamned green leather-bound spelling book!" She slammed her fist on the bedside stand and a glass of water crashed to the floor.

"You and Miss Mary Lou Elliot!" Minnie cried. "You get out of here! I've got things to do with this fool bag!"

When the time came, Miss Oxford grew less and less sure how she felt about the three of them living together. She decided to give it some good solid thought one Saturday morning while she cleaned her apartment in the nurses' quarters. The heart of the matter was sex all right, she concluded, and the thought sent a shiver up her spine. And then she experienced her first feelings of jealousy, which she felt as a mild tachycardia. Oh dear, I am going to be sick and die before my time, she thought. She sat down for a while and her symptoms passed, but her thoughts about the three patients persisted, such as: if sex is at the bottom of it, then who . . . and how. Warren was paralyzed and the other two were so strange and ugly. She tried to make them appear foolish in her mind, and when she failed at this, she tried to malign first their intelligence and then their motivation. But none of this worked.

Later she had to admit to herself: *I want to go with them.*

When she got back to the hospital on Monday and heard they were truly leaving Wednesday, she could not manage her feelings very well and she was unusually severe with the orderly and with Miss Holt and with a new patient who had just been admitted to the floor.

"I think you might want to consider the psychosomatic components of your illness," she said sternly to the new patient, who was a mild young man with two broken legs he had sustained in a thirty-foot fall from the side of a building.

"Oh Jesus," Miss Holt said under her breath.

Miss Oxford then turned full blast on Miss Holt and accused her of having seduced a young medical student at a staff party.

"But that was two years ago!" Miss Holt said, smiling as she remembered how pleasant it had been.

Warren sat blinking at the resident and tried to control an impulse to say something fresh. The resident had small hands and feet like a girl's and he tried to minimize them by speaking in a loud and manly voice.

"I'm sending you out on Gantrisin," he announced. "Keep the old pipes clean."

"Yessireee," Warren said.

The resident looked closely to see if Warren were putting him on, but he couldn't decide. He then outlined the precautions against a contaminated urinary tract. Warren was not listening—he was thinking of Guiles. Guiles had long fine hands dusted with long fine black hairs. Guiles filed his nails continually, shaping them, shaping them. His feet were as delicate as wasps, and in the wintertime, when no one could see, he painted his toenails, one foot gold and the other silver.

"I will now read to you from *The Conquest of Mexico*," Guiles would say, placing the plate of sandwiches between them on the couch.

"If you notice the urine becoming cloudy," the resident was saying, "that's a danger signal."

"It is important that you know about Mexico," Guiles would say, "because it tells what happened to a proud but stupid people."

"You might also notice an elevation in temperature," the resident said.

"Or at least we have come to call them stupid," Guiles said, "because they got conquered. If this had not happened, they might have turned north and hounded the American Indian."

"If the temperature persists for say two or three days, call the clinic and take the pills."

"However, the Spanish precluded this possibility. Please eat your sandwich—you are looking thin."

Guiles!

"By the way," said the resident, "I noticed in your chart that you were shot when you were a young boy vacationing in Provincetown."

"Yes," Warren said quickly, and started from the room.

The resident detained him: "I've been to Provincetown a couple of times. Pretty racy, eh?" The resident winked awkwardly.

"Yessiree," Warren said, winking back. He knew as if by radar that the resident had in his mind to dicuss how Warren had been shot, and this made Warren uneasy.

"Do you remember much about your accident?" the resident said.

"Nothing," Warren said. "Nothing at all." He pivoted his wheelchair as though it were jet-powered and wheeled swiftly off down the hall.

"Goodbye, goodbye," Minnie called.

"Hush," Junie Moon said. "It's the middle of the night. We're not going yet."

"I'll wave until you are out of sight—until you are three dots on the horizon."

"All right."

"I used to go down to the depot," Minnie said, "to watch the noonday train and to do a little waving. I knew there would be people aboard who had no one and they'd just as leave wave to me. I never had a parasol, but I took my daddy's big black umbrella. That did better than any flimsy old parasol for keeping off the sun. I didn't care if they laughed."

"Why did you go at noonday? Why not early morning or in the cool evening?"

"Because there's something special about the noonday train. It's already been a long way and it has a long way to go. And besides, William B. Jackson was on duty in the Railway Express office and I had a case on him. I was crazy about that man and there wasn't a thing to recommend him. He would sit in the old yellow depot all day making out those yellow Railway Express forms for big boxes going some place. He worked with a soft lead pencil, printing out the forms in his big square letters. He was the most near-sighted man that ever lived, and why the Railway Express hired him, I'll never know. He wore a green sun visor and an orange vest and he was as skinny as a bird. As I say, he had little to recommend him, but I liked him just the same."

"It's hard to tell who you'll end up liking," Junie Moon said.

"Oh, I didn't end up liking him. It was more like I started out that way and stopped. He was very funny with girls and would do things like grabbing them where he didn't really mean to and then laughing in a silly way. Or he would say rude things that he hadn't meant to be rude. His silly mistakes ended up giving me a headache, so I quit going to the depot."

"Did he miss you?"

"I don't know, because I never heard one way or the other. But one thing that's funny. I never hear a noon whistle without thinking about William B. Jackson—wherever he may be now."

"Sometimes I think of people I haven't seen for a long time," Junie Moon said. "I'll be going along and all of a sudden into my mind pops Alex Whittaker or Janice Fiste—for no reason at all. And then I get to thinking: wouldn't they be surprised to know that old Junie Moon, whom they hadn't seen for twenty years and whom they didn't know very well even then, was walking along the street thinking about them."

"People come and go too much," Minnie said.

"Some people have to move along, Minnie."

"Who said so?" Minnie snapped.

"You'd better go to sleep now."

"That's all I do—sleep, sleep, sleep! What's so all-fire good about sleeping, I'd like to know? My great grandfather

Davis slept only three hours a night and he lived to be one hundred and one and a half. What do you think of that?"

"I think that's fine, Minnie." Junie Moon was being drugged with a creeping kind of sleepiness which she tried to fight off. She could feel the back of her brain going numb and she hoped that Minnie wouldn't notice.

"Grandpa Davis used to get up at three in the morning and write down his recollections."

Minnie's voice was fading in and out of Junie Moon's mind and she was hearing only every other word. She tried shaking her head to wake up, but she hadn't the energy. The only way she could convince Minnie that she was still awake was to answer her.

"He was really quite remarkable," Junie Moon said.

"Yes, indeed," said Minnie. "Bright as a button."

Junie Moon made another effort: "There were twenty-five bales, as I recall."

"What?" Minnie said.

Oh Lord, thought Junie Moon, I dozed off and said something silly. She would try to make sense out of it before Minnie became suspicious.

"Twenty-five railroad trains," she said hopefully.

But Minnie caught her. "You were drifting off, Junie Moon," she said, "right in the middle of something I was telling you."

Minnie waved goodbye but she was not close enough to the window to see the taxicab. She had asked an orderly to move her, but by the time he got around to it, they were gone.

They left at two o'clock in a taxicab. They went off with two shopping bags which contained all their earthly possessions.

The resident with the clean lips paused in the midst of his medical duties and watched them go.

"Goodbye," he called, but they didn't hear him. He thought it was just as well because he wouldn't know what to say after goodbye.

Miss Oxford pried open a window on the sun porch with a clean scalpel and watched them leave from there. Miss Holt saw her and was about to give her a good ribbing, but she changed her mind. Anybody with such tiny breasts and such big feet deserved to be let alone, she thought.

Warren rode in the front with the driver and directed him where to go and exactly how to get there. He opened the window and the wind blew his blond beard, giving him a rakish look. Junie Moon sat in a corner and looked at her knees. She had not failed to notice that the cab driver had gasped and looked pale when he had seen her face. She knew he would be grabbing looks at her in the rear-view mirror. Arthur sat beside her, looking grim and straight ahead. Actually he was trying to control what he thought was an approaching seizure, which turned out only to be nervousness. When he realized this, he tentatively reached across and touched Junie Moon's hand. He did not mind the feel of it, and he thought he saw her try to smile.

Ten

Sidney Wyner wore a dirty sleeveless undershirt most of the time when he was home. His wife complained about this, but it did her no good. Sidney knew that he was unattractive in the undershirt and that everybody, from his wife to the newspaper boy, hated it, but he wore it anyway, as if he had a grudge against the world.

When the taxicab pulled up next door, Sidney was mowing his lawn. He was home at that hour because he was on vacation, and he was mowing the lawn because his lazy son Fred would not get out of bed and find a job, let alone cut the grass. Sidney hated his son and vowed he would kill him, but somehow he never got around to it. Instead, he used his energy butting into other people's business and collecting little items of gossip about them which he would use in mean and hateful ways. Furthermore, he looked mean. He had narrow lips which he sucked back over terrible teeth, looking as if he were about to snap, and his eyes were flat and almost totally without brows or lashes. The sleeveless undershirt completed the picture.

"Jesus Christ," he said, grinning and licking his terrible teeth as the doors to the cab opened and the three of them got out with their two shopping bags. "Would you look at that!" Then he called to his wife: "Hey, Lil, get the hell out here and see what I see."

Watching Sidney Wyner from his perch in the banyan tree next door was a large horned owl. The banyan tree was like a forest in itself, with air roots that ran to the ground and back up again, and in the center of all the leaves and branches it was cool and dark, even in the middle of a hot summer day. The owl was not really watching Sidney but instead had fixed his eyes on him and found that the man's slow movements back and forth across the lawn were rest-ful. From his perch he could see into his own yard as well. He had claimed the tree several years ago when the little house beneath it became abandoned and the vines and weeds began to grow and mice and other juicy edibles came to live there. For the owl it meant not having to fly too far for a quick meal, something he hated to do when the weather grew hot. Although other birds and small animals lived in the tree too, it essentially belonged to the owl since he was by far the largest and the most formidable-looking, with his bright yellow eyes and his sharp feathered ears. Unfortu-nately, small boys in the neighborhood learned of the owl's roosting place and sometimes would come with rocks or BB guns to try to rout him. But so far the owl had escaped with only the loss of a few feathers.

When Sidney Wyner's attention turned to the taxicab, so did the owl's. The owl cocked his head to one side as the three people stood before *his* house, *his* yard, and finally entered *his* gate.

Junie Moon looked at the house and thought: Oh dear God. Arthur stared over her shoulder into the tangled yard. There had once been a path from the sidewalk to the entryway, but now it was knotted with weeds laced through with orange nasturtiums. It was difficult to see the house because grapevines had escaped their trellis and circled it in a stranglehold. Two windows were broken and a smattering of bricks lay on the roof as if a large bird had dropped them.

For a moment Warren's face showed stunned surprise, but this quickly passed. He had already seen the possibilities.

"Isn't it marvelous?" he said. "Get a load of that tree." He tried to navigate the path in his wheelchair but the growth was too thick, so he thrashed at the bushes with a stick to clear himself a way. "Nothing to it," he said, his face flushed with exertion. "Well, don't just stand there. Help me!"

They helped him to the door and the key was in the mailbox except the lock was so rusty it wouldn't open. Arthur went in through a window and opened the back door and they sat down in the kitchen on two rickety chairs, looking at a non-electric icebox and a part-wood, part-gas stove and a sink that stood on three silly, high legs, and a window that was completely grown over with grapevines and wild roses. And it was so dark with all this and being under the banyan tree that they had to strike matches to see.

After a while Junie Moon went into the back yard and sat

down under the tree. For the moment she did not want to think of the present. She thought instead of where she had lived with her mother and daddy in a house built under a tree, or perhaps the tree had been planted and grew up to cover the house. That tree came up out of the ground in two huge trunks and looked as though a giant had been buried head first in the ground with only his legs exposed. Once she and her friends discovered this image, they giggled and made up games about the giant as they played in the crotch.

"Look at me," one would cry. "I'm going to give him a big pinch!" And they would shriek.

"I'm going to do something worse!" another would say, and they would have a whispered conference.

And then, gales of laughter, ending in helpless tears.

"Oh, Junie Moon, you're dirty!"

She smiled, remembering. One year the tree had bloomed and the scent was so strong that her daddy had greeted people at the door with: "Come in! It's Saturday night at the whorehouse!" That sweet terrible smell got into everything —even the food.

"We can't stay here," Arthur said, joining her in the yard.

"Why not?" she said.

"Because the house is falling down. And it's not like Warren said it would be."

Junie Moon laughed. "Don't you know by now that nothing is like he says?"

"It doesn't have a porch."

"It has a tree. You'll have to admit this is some tree." She looked up into the tall branches and saw the owl.

"And it has a hooty owl," she said. "That's a good-luck omen."

"Who said so?"

"I did."

"We will have to haul the ice," he said.

"That's all right."

"But what will we haul it in, I'd like to know?"

"We'll find something."

"What?" His eyes were filling with tears but he didn't know why.

"We'll get a wagon. A little kid's wagon would do the trick."

"Where will we get that?" His voice was trembling.

"How the hell should I know, Arthur," she said. "From a little kid, I suppose."

Arthur walked quickly back into the house.

It was then Junie Moon noticed that Sidney Wyner had been watching over the next-door hedge. She saw his lips pulled back over his yellow teeth, forming a wicked smile. She walked directly toward him, or as directly as she could since the brambles were so thick.

"Hoot, hoot, hooooo," she cried at him. "Hoot, hoot, hooooo."

Sidney Wyner looked aghast and ran.

Later that day Binnie Farber came to call. She came in a car that looked like an old dustbin, shrugged her shoulders when she saw the house, and struggled up the path with a cardboard carton and three paper bags. The first thing they need, she said to herself, is a machete.

The bags, as it turned out, contained food, a can opener, bed linen, a French cookbook, three towels, soap, and a quart of beer, among other things. "Here comes Lady Bountiful," she said, "come to look after the deserving poor. Leave it to you," she said to Warren, "to find a place with atmosphere."

He beamed. The secret of his success with Binnie Farber was to play straight to her irony.

"But what will happen to us when this food is gone?" Warren said.

She took a check from her purse but passed it beyond his outstretched hand to Junie Moon. "You'll be sent a check twice a month," she said, and then she told them about a number of rigmaroles and procedures for receiving public assistance. During this explanation Arthur turned his back on them and faced the wall.

"He doesn't like the idea of charity," Junie Moon said.

"I love it," Warren said.

"He was humiliated by it when he was a boy," Junie Moon said, wishing that Arthur would at least turn and look at them.

"I receive a small gratuity each month," Warren said. "I look at it as a little monthly surprise!"

"You'd better put your little surprise in the common pot," Binnie Farber said.

"Certainly not," he replied. "It's too small to share."

And then, as if to hide his stinginess, he made some boiled coffee and set out cookies from the paper bag onto a pie pan which he decorated with a piece of yellow tissue paper.

"The first of many galas," he said, turning Arthur around so that he was facing them. "The next time you come, we will have iced tea in the garden."

"Ho!" said Junie Moon.

Binnie Farber left at about a quarter to four. Arthur went with her to the gate and Warren and Junie Moon waved from the door. When the car drove away, Arthur walked slowly back to the house and they sat down again in the kitchen. Warren chattered without stopping for an hour about Binnie Farber, speculating about her sex life, her figure, her past, present, and future. He was highly critical of her, but he would not permit them to be. When he finally ran down, they sat in silence in the dark room. Warren looked at the ceiling as though his mind were far away. Arthur looked at Junie Moon's face and was surprised that the revulsion he used to feel seemed to be fading. Junie Moon stared at her hands. She was wondering where she could find a child's wagon for hauling the ice.

Eleven

No one could say exactly why the fighting started, but it was soon and quickly bitter. Between the men it went in sharp stabs designed to hit open nerves. With Junie Moon, who could deflect an attack and send it whistling over her head, the laceration was only postponed, because on the return carom she placed herself directly in front of the barrage. In that way, she was a glutton.

Warren had tried to make order, but his attempts fell flat. "We should put our heads together and devise a planned economy," he said, shortly after Binnie Farber left.

Arthur was hot and tired. "Your planning a little dinner would be more to the point," he snapped.

It began slowly from this point on—a disagreement as to how the can opener worked, whether or not the beans should be heated in or out of the can, if the stove had a pilot light.

"You will blow us all to kingdom come," Warren said.

At first Junie Moon stayed out of it, not even listening as she wandered through the house deciding which room she wanted for herself. ("We will draw straws," Warren had said, but she and Arthur had voted him down, saying that was too babyish. Now she wished they had done it and settled the matter.) She could hear their voices growing shrill with anger, but the words were muffled. She remembered her parents arguing like that in their bedroom and she had always wanted to listen—to peek and listen—but she never had the nerve.

While the argument grew more heated in the kitchen, she unpacked her shopping bag. All her personal items fitted into one corner of a dresser drawer. Junie Moon was a fierce anti-collector, disposing of things almost as quickly as she acquired them, as if they contained a deadly serum. She had no favorite locket or hand-painted cup or decoration of any kind except a sachet pillow she had once bought at a resort which said on it: *This pillow is filled with genuine mountain heather*. She had two sets of underwear including one she wore, three dresses, one pair of shoes, and a bathrobe. She had a red plastic purse in which she carried all her cosmetic items, none of which she had been able to use since her injury. She carried her toothbrush knotted in a handkerchief in the pocket of her raincoat. These things comprised her entire belongings. When any of the items wore out, she replaced them as closely as she could with the identical article.

She unpacked the things and spread a blanket over the hard mattress and lay down in a room that had yellow flowered wallpaper. For the first time, and to the accompaniment of the fighting going on in the kitchen, she allowed herself to wonder what had happened to her mother and daddy who had moved away and had never come to see her in the hospital. "Goddamn you both," she said aloud, but in her mind's eye she could see her father's pained, weak mouth turning down at the corners as he searched for an explanation. She thought he might have said: "It had nothing to do with you, babe. You know your mother. She got restless and had to move on."

Liar!

They ran off and joined Arthur's parents, that's what they did. All of them—all of the runaway daddies and itchy-footed mamas were living in a run-down campground next to the ocean. She hoped the wind would never stop blowing where they were. She hoped it would blow the sand into their eyes and their food and their beds and that the sun would turn everything pale for them. They would live worse than gypsies, hungry and with flies nesting in their eyes—and that would serve them right for their mean unloving ways. She hoped the buzzards would circle over their camp every day at noon—just to remind them.

Having thought this, she felt better and joined the men in the kitchen. They were still fighting and she decided to join in, making little comments from time to time to fan the flames.

They fought for almost a week until they were pale and exhausted. At first it was because they were afraid of having to tend to their ailments by themselves without Miss Oxford picking at them. Without knowing it, they missed the lack

of privacy of the hospital. Their bodies and thoughts had
been exposed for so long for many and all to see, it was hard
to stitch them up again into belonging only to them. It was
like reorganizing the house after a long and arduous party.

Then, as this passed, and they became more sure, they
fought because of who they were. "I am living with freaks,"
each of them announced at one time or another. And each of
them feared he was the biggest freak. It was not their dream
to be this way. There was no magazine printed that pictured
three people like themselves living together in a run-down
bungalow under an oppressive tree.

Then they fought because they were getting used to each
other, and the insults began to have a more tailored sting to
them. Later they fought because they were getting close,
but that was quite different.

One day Junie Moon said, "I cannot stand your damned
bickering another minute," and she jammed on a large Mexican sombrero which she had found in a back closet and
loped off down the street.

"Now you've done it," Warren yelled.

Arthur shook with rage.

She did not look to the right or to the left and she went
along at a great clip with her hands tucked behind her back
and the sombrero hiding her face. The town was hot and
still in the middle of the day and occasionally a child would
look up from what he was doing on his front lawn and
watch her until she was out of sight. Sidney Wyner
watched her from his garage, where he was trying to hammer straight an old brass curtain rod. He had been able to
hear most of the arguing next door by working on his hedge

on that side of the yard, and he would come in and tell his wife about it, for the most part exaggerating what he had heard, and embellishing it here and there so that it could be told properly. He had almost, but not quite, decided that Arthur was some kind of a sexual pervert. He would take a long and tantalizing time deciding which kind.

"Why don't you call the cops if their fighting bothers you so much," Mrs. Wyner said to her husband.

"Yeah, I'll do that." But he had no intention whatsoever of trying to stop it.

He watched Junie Moon go down the street and a little later he put a shirt over his dirty underwear and followed her.

Junie Moon passed the post office to where the town began to pick up. The signs and billboards grew thicker but for the most part they were short and to the point like BEER and EAT and SHOES. There were lots of empty parking places at the curb and many of the storeowners were sitting on canvas chairs out in front, fanning themselves or talking with their friends. Business was poor at that hour. One of the shopkeepers got a glimpse of Junie Moon's face. He said "Jesus!" in a soft, almost affectionate way. Then he stood up and looked after her, scratching his behind as if he could not believe what he saw.

She passed Sloan's ice-cream store and had a sudden longing to eat a hot butterscotch sundae with lots of whipped cream and pecans, but she was afraid to go in. It would cost too much, she said to herself. What she meant was that she was not yet ready to eat in a public place.

When she passed the fish market, a man with long mustaches who was scaling a large gray fish looked straight at her face and waved with his knife. She waved back and she noticed that he looked hard at her hands too, but without apparent shock. Maybe it was easier for him, she thought, because all day he cut and chopped and scaled and degutted. She would go into that store soon, she thought, and make the man's acquaintance, because he had been the first stranger she had seen since the accident who looked like he might not mind.

On the next block she found a hardware store and went in to price toy wagons. They were very expensive and they had fat pneumatic tires and chrome bumpers and headlights which ran on batteries. There was no such thing as a simple wagon for scooting or hauling.

"Good afternoon, madam."

The voice came from behind her, boxing her into a corner.

"Can I show you a wagon?"

"That's all right," she said, not turning around. "I'm just looking."

"How old is the child?" the salesman said.

"Fifty," she whispered, but he did not hear.

"Did you see a woman with a torn-up face come by here wearing a Mexican sombrero?" Sidney Wyner asked everyone sitting on the sidewalk.

"I seen her," a man finally said. "Who is she?"

"Some whore," he said to the man. "Probably just got sprung for good behavior, if you know what I mean." He winked at the man and went on his way. He felt a dampness in his armpits as though he were on the verge of a wonderful adventure. He often interpreted these autonomic symptoms as indications of his sexual cunning. Of course she is a whore, he said to himself. Why else would she be living with two men, and undoubtedly married to neither of them.

He found her at last at the hardware store. He stared through the window, but she didn't notice him. He waved first one hand and then the other. He jumped up and down on the sidewalk and waggled his hands at his ears and stuck out his tongue. His behavior startled even himself, but he could not seem to control it.

The salesman looked up and saw him and said quickly to Junie Moon: "We have other models in the back."

"Are they cheaper?"

"Why don't we go back there and take a look?" he said.

"Yes," she said. "Why don't we?"

And he propelled her out of sight of the foolish man outside the window.

"Whew!" Mario said to himself as he slit the fish up the middle, scooped out the insides, and threw them into a pail. He could not get Junie Moon's face to leave his mind. She reminded him of his grandmother, who was the only member of his smooth-skinned family with any sort of a physical flaw. She had disfigured her right arm with a pot of boiling soup which slipped from the stove, but instead of being ashamed of it, she wore it like a banner, waving attention to it and shouting out the story to anyone who would listen . . . "Then the cauldron crashed from the stove, pouring a fountain of soup like lava from Mount Etna. I was being punished for some sin," she would say, her eyes narrowing with mystery. "Can you guess what it was?" And through the years they guessed and guessed, but they never struck upon the right sin. Of course Mario's grandmother had had only one arm affected, but because of that, he was more curious than disgusted by the sight of Junie Moon. He hoped she would walk by again so he could wave and perhaps call out a greeting.

When the wagon salesman finally saw Junie Moon's face, his heart filled with anguish. It was as though he had found a smashed kitten in the road, and yet he did not want to get blood on his clean suit. "Oh Lord," he said to himself. "Oh Lord, oh Lord, oh Lord." He sold her a wagon for half what it cost. He did this without knowing it, but she said nothing. She felt sorry for the salesman and wanted very much to pat his hand—a gesture she often used with men in the days before the accident—but she knew this would frighten him to death. So instead she pulled her hat down over her eyes and tried to make a joke.

"Maybe I could get a paper route with this thing," she said, indicating the wagon.

"Oh, you wouldn't have to do that," the salesman said quickly, fearing that at any moment he might cry.

"A milk route?" she giggled.

But his eyes were so sad she turned and left the store, dragging the wagon behind her.

"We've decided to have a party," Warren said when Junie Moon returned.

"I'm glad you came back," Arthur said.

"I've been making brownies," Warren said. "Don't they smell heavenly?"

"We were afraid you had gotten so mad you went away for good," Arthur said.

"We will have brownies and some cooling lemonade out under the tree after supper," Warren said.

"We agreed that our behavior has been abominable," Arthur said, slipping the sombrero off Junie Moon's head and putting it on his own. "Do I look like Cesar Romero?" The headband was still warm from her hair and he felt a sudden intimacy.

"You look like Baby Dumpling without his Live Animal Act," Warren said.

"I'm tired of fighting," Arthur said, "so don't waste your breath."

"Sorry," Warren said. "I forgot we had made a truce." He opened the door of the ancient oven and took out a tray of brownies. "I may bake bread next week." He smiled like a delighted child.

"We arrived at a truce," Arthur said, "because we were afraid of losing you."

"She knows that!" Warren said, suddenly petulant.

But Arthur persisted: "Without you, there wouldn't be any point to it."

Junie Moon looked from one to the other. She was getting so used to them she was beginning to forget what they looked like. Even when she saw them from a few feet away it was hard to remember because her feelings washed over their features and changed them as the tide changes the sand.

"I'm glad you arrived at a truce," she said, trying to ignore the love in their voices. She could not cope with it because she had not yet gotten over her trip into town. "I have a very low tolerance to fighting in any form," she said, taking a brownie and breaking it into three pieces. "I find yelling particularly annoying." She popped the pieces into their mouths and cooled one for herself in the palm of her hand. "Yelling reminds me of bleeding and I've had enough of that for one lifetime."

"Taste it, taste it!" Warren said.

She put the brownie into her mouth and looked at him through narrowed eyes. "You are a mean brownie maker," she said and he flushed with pleasure.

Later they sat under the tree and had their party and listened to the night sounds. The tree fell around them like a blanket. The owl stirred above them, sending down a tiny shower of twigs. A frog. A cricket. A dog barked.

"Sing us a song, Junie Moon," Arthur said.

She surprised herself: "Sure." She could not remember singing since she sang silly songs in junior high school and even then her voice never sounded as if it belonged to her. But now she leaned back and stared up through the tree to the dark stars and her voice was as high and clear as a flute:

*"As a blackbird in the spring,
    Beneath the willow tree,
    Sat and piped, I heard him sing,
    Singing Ora Lee."*

Twelve

The trouble began with Warren as it usually did—innocently. In his never-ending search for Guiles, he raced through the years looking into the faces of everyone—man, woman, and child—and then, not finding Guiles, he would try to re-create him out of anyone who would stand for it. From time to time some person bent on his own destructive course, and seeing Warren searching in this way, would detain him and damage him. This was not to say that Warren disliked it.

Shortly after they moved into the house he began bringing home people. The first was a young feeble-minded boy named Jerry who helped deliver milk and who picked his nose. He came into the kitchen and looked silently at the three of them. Then he snickered and ran. The next was a

Tell me

Mr. Jamison who belonged to the local archery club. He saw it as his civic duty to assist Warren home from downtown, and he came huffing in from the hot noonday sun, pushing Warren's wheelchair with one hand and mopping his face with the other. Warren offered him some lemonade Junie Moon was fixing at the sink. He sat down, still mopping, and saying "boy, oh boy" over and over again. But when he saw Junie Moon's face Mr. Jamison made a sound as if all the wind had been kicked out of him and he excused himself.

The next person to come was a beautiful young woman with long, spun-silver hair. She did everything that bad girls do in the movies: she smoked and drank too much, she drove too fast with the top down, and she got involved with gangsters or people like Warren who could not defend themselves. She gave the illusion of being intelligent and mysterious, but she was neither. Her life was so distractible and distracting, however, that no one cared much about her virtues.

She ordered Warren about as if he were a stupid servant, and she took him to expensive places to eat and told him about her house which was like a castle on the side of the mountain. About this house, in which she reputedly lived alone with a dozen real servants, had sprung many legends and wild stories and downright lies. A man was supposed to guard the place with a shotgun, but he had not been entirely successful, for it was the favorite sport of some people in town—especially the young boys—to try to peep into the windows and see what was going on. Their stories varied so much it was hard to tell who was telling the truth, but one thing was constant: the scenes described were not run-of-the-mill.

The first day Warren brought this girl home (or rather, she brought *him* home, screeching up the street with the top down and the radio blaring) was shortly after four on a hot Wednesday. Their laughing and the racket from the car radio brought Sidney Wyner flying to the hedge, where he stood and stared unabashedly. Junie Moon and Arthur were having a tuna sandwich under the tree and barely noticed them come in since Warren had been dragging so many people home.

"This is Gregory," he said, introducing her as if she were a prize.

Arthur struggled to his feet. He wanted to make a joke and say "Gregory Peck?" but he didn't have the nerve. Instead, he shook her hand and offered her the orange crate he had been sitting on. The girl had pale green eyes which made Arthur nervous, and without even thinking, he put his hand lightly on Junie Moon's shoulder as if this kept them free and clear of her. Gregory ignored the orange crate and sat in the lap of the big tree's roots, running her bare feet through the dust and humming a tune to herself. Warren chattered as if he had known her for years, telling Arthur and Junie Moon about the precise place in town where they had met and what they had done thereafter, minute by minute.

Finally Gregory said, "Shut up, Warren," without even looking up.

"Of course, darling," Warren said, looking as though she had paid him an extravagant compliment. They sat in silence for a while, but then Junie Moon said to Arthur, "I don't think she meant us," and she laughed softly and passed Arthur the rest of his sandwich.

"Would you like something to eat?" Arthur asked Gregory. He was beginning to see how beautiful she was and to envy Warren his talent for picking up people.

Gregory did not answer, but instead turned and walked quickly through the brambles to the hedge, behind which Sidney Wyner was standing.

"Get the goddamned hell out of here," she said to him. Sidney Wyner emitted a little cry as if he had been switched on his bare legs.

When she turned back to them, her face was radiant.

"I hate Peeping Toms," she said. "In Bonassola once, a young girl took off her bathing suit at the beach and walked home naked through the town and nobody paid much attention. However, the police had to fight the men away from the windows of her cottage at night—young men to whom being naked only counted if it occurred indoors in private."

"People spy on Gregory all the time," Warren said with pride.

"That's my problem too," Junie Moon said with a harsh laugh. "But for different reasons."

"I'm not sure they're different," Gregory said, looking hard at Junie Moon's face.

Warren hoped the two of them would get along. He didn't worry about Arthur, but it was important that Junie Moon accept Gregory and appreciate her importance without being her usual sarcastic self. Already he had begun to imitate some of Gregory's mannerisms, he liked her that much.

"Gregory has three men patrolling her property, just to keep away the undesirables," he said to Junie Moon, holding his head slightly to the side the way Gregory did.

"Only one," Gregory said. Then she turned suddenly to Junie Moon, as if she had formulated a plan. "Why don't you all come home with me. We will take a swim and have dinner on the terrace."

"I am bad enough in this outfit with most of me covered up," Junie Moon said, "let alone parading around in a bathing suit."

"I have seizures sometimes, and I can't swim," Arthur said, as though he were protecting Junie Moon.

"Anything else?" Gregory said.

"What?" said Junie Moon.

"Any other deformity, disability, limitation, or disease process which you care to cite before considering my invitation?" Her voice was tough, but she smiled and that cut through everything. Junie Moon had to laugh and that settled it. They all got into Gregory's car, Warren sitting in the front, his beard blowing back over his shoulder, while Junie Moon with her sombrero, and Arthur, sat in the back.

Gregory pointed the nose of the big car around the final curve and from there they could hear music coming from an upper window of the house. It sounded like an old-fashioned dance band, muffled, as if it were coming across a lake on a summer night. The house was huge. And it was bright and extravagant.

Gregory slowed the car, and a small, dark-skinned man emerged from a path beside the road and rode the rest of the way to the house on the front fender.

They were taken to a room which was half indoors and half out and bounded by a pool with shade trees and soft lounging chairs. Warren wheeled across the floor at top speed, seeing everything. There were platters of food and bathing suits and towels and hats and lotions on a tray. The music sounded stronger but sadder now because of a wailing saxophone.

"It's gorgeous," Warren cried, skidding to a stop in front of Gregory.

"Please amuse yourselves," Gregory said, giving Arthur and Junie Moon a curious smile. She started from the room, pushing Warren's chair.

Junie Moon was alarmed. "Where are you taking him?" she cried.

Gregory laughed. "For a walk," she said.

"I don't like it here," Arthur said, after they had gone.

"It's all right," Junie Moon said. "Gregory is the kind who likes to put people on."

"That's what scares me. It makes me think I may be going to have a seizure."

"You may be, but lie down in the shade first. It makes it easier for me to look after you. I'll make you a pink Razz-a-ma-tazz," she said, going to the bar beside the pool.

He stretched out on a lounge and closed his eyes.

"Only twenty-five to a customer," she said. "And that's a rule to be observed!" Then she mixed the drink, pouring into tall glasses from most of the bottles on the bar, singing a little song: *Wait until you sip the Razz-a-ma-tazz, it will make you want to do the purple Ga-zazz.* She put in orange and cherries and mint until the glasses looked like fruit salad, and she thrust one into Arthur's hand.

"A person just might get to like this kind of a life," she said, dancing around the edge of the pool. "Junie Moon at the Ritz . . . Junie Moon and Her Black Ferrari." She took little bites of the sandwiches and replaced them on the tray, smiling at her extravagance. She held a bikini next to her lean frame, and tried to imagine herself in it. (Her only bathing suit had been black wool, with cutouts under the arms.) "Junie Moon Takes the Plunge." She bent down and opened one of Arthur's eyes. "I know you're in there," she said. "Drink up and forget your troubles."

The old-fashioned dance band was playing a waltz from *The Red Mill* and it reminded her of a tow-headed boy she had met one summer. Howard Young. Junie Moon, why don't you ask your mama to get you a permanent wave? He always had a thin film of sweat on his upper lip, and across the years came the taste of it. You ought to wipe your lip before you kiss a girl, Howard. And you ought to get a permanent wave and maybe get your teeth straightened, Junie Moon. If your teeth were straightened, you wouldn't notice my sweaty lip, lemme show you. Then he had kissed her until it wasn't fun any more.

The reflection of her own face rippled over the dark water. "Junie Moon and Her Rude Awakening," she called. No one answered. A wind stirred the trees, but that was the only sound. She made herself another Razz-a-ma-tazz and sat down on the lounge next to Arthur. He twisted in his sleep and she arranged his head in her lap, pushing his dark hair back from his forehead. Never mind, Howard Young, she thought, you're probably working in some filthy gas station out in the middle of nowhere. And besides, if I had wanted a permanent wave, my mama would have gotten me one. Poor Mama. She would have liked this house. The ones they had lived in had been little more than shacks, paper thin so that sounds carried from one room to the next, with windows that leaked cold air in the winter. Thin houses that baked in the summer. "Wait and see," Mama would say. "Some day we'll find us a fancy old palacio with gold-plated doorknobs and five bathtubs." Itchy-footed Mama was still looking. *Dear Mama, well here I am in that palacio of yours and it's just like you said it would be only more so.* Junie Moon never wrote to her mama because she had no idea where to send the letters, but sometimes she made up letters—or actually postcards—that she might have sent. She always ended them by saying "Write soon" and signed them "Your obedient daughter, Junie Moon," which she thought was very elegant without being sentimental. She supposed, if she were writing, she should mention Gregory, but she could not think of what to say. *But getting back to the palacio* . . . Junie Moon decided to go and see for herself.

The corridors were wide, with Spanish tiles on the floor and high, open beams. On either side were the grand rooms done in French and Spanish periods, each as perfect and cold as a museum. Junie Moon sat at the end of a long banquet table and tried to imagine the three of them eating there. "Pass the ketchup, lambie," she said, giggling, but her voice was lost in the tapestries and she ran from the room and down the hall. The kitchen was bigger than the entire house under the banyan tree, and there two cooks, a serving maid, and a butler played cards around a porcelain table while the houseboy kept score. They looked as carefully chosen as the furniture. The houseboy was the first to notice her and he jumped to his feet, making a little bow. "May we help you, madame?" he said. The others looked up, but then quickly back to their cards. It would be hard to tell, she thought, whether they looked away because of the sight of me or because of their card game. She lifted her hand in a kind of wave and went on her way. The corridor curved past a library and opened onto a terrace which overlooked the lights of the town. Junie Moon leaned against the stone and listened to the night sounds. Her lighthearted mood had vanished. She thought that despite all its magnificent furnishings, the house was as empty as a ship at sea with no one aboard. She felt a chill, even though the night was warm, and she hurried back through the house to find Arthur.

As she neared the swimming pool, she heard the scream.

Arthur had heard it too, and sat up blinking. "What was that?"

They stared at each other, both of them trying to pretend they didn't know what it was.

"It was the wind," Junie Moon said.

"No," said Arthur, "it was more like a dog baying."

They waited in silence, but the cry did not come again.

"Let's go home now, Arthur," Junie Moon said.

"It may have been an airplane," he said. "Sometimes jet planes make a whining noise, like a man. At any rate, we can't go home without Warren."

Junie Moon's voice was shrill. "Warren can take care of himself."

"You've got to admit that sounded like Warren," Arthur said finally.

"I guess so," she said, sighing.

They went down the hallway to find him.

Far down the long corridors, past the endless grand rooms that made up Gregory's house, in a bare, monk-like cell set aside from the main house by its own ramp, Warren sat weeping.

"The game room," Gregory had said.

"But it's empty. I don't see any games."

"You must use your imagination, darling."

Warren usually wept because of frustration or self-pity. He had never known real tears of mourning because his only loss—Guiles—had been minimized by his tight-lipped, scientific grandmother. ("There's a good little man—no tears for something you can't remedy.") Now he wept because he could not do the one thing that would endear him to Gregory, perhaps even make her want to keep him with her forever. He thought: Life will pass me by because I am a cripple. I will spend all my days going from one place to the next looking for a friend. The Wandering Jew. The Man without a Country. Rolling off into the sunset in a wheelchair. Nobody cares, nobody cares.

The crying refreshed him and he blew his nose. He would try again. This time it might work. He smiled faintly at Gregory, who sat opposite him. How hard it was to tell what she was thinking. The light from the single overhead bulb shone down on her silver hair. Instead of her usual half-annoyed expression, her features were sharply focused, adding to her beauty. Warren had to admit, however, that she frightened him. It was probably her eyes, he thought. They were as narrow and glittering as an animal's.

"No more screaming," Gregory said. "Either you try or you don't. Nobody is forcing you to stay here, you know."

"I'm sorry," Warren said, mopping up his tears.

Arthur and Junie Moon had found them by following the sound of their voices. The door was ajar and they stood outside in the darkness, watching.

"It's nonsense to say that you can't walk," Gregory said. "Psychogenic."

"I suppose so," Warren said weakly.

"I will count to ten once more and this time you will do it." She rose and circled him, her body as taut, her manner as commanding as a lion tamer.

Arthur made a motion to enter the room, but Junie Moon restrained him. She was sick with sorrow for Warren, that he would go to such lengths with this woman, but she found she could not interrupt it. It was like a terrible side show. Watch the man with strong arms and the yellow beard fall down on the floor. Sprawl flat on his face. Watch the lady smile. Listen to her laugh. Which lady? Junie Moon shuddered.

Gregory finished counting to ten. "All right, my little pet, my little half-man, my little darling . . ." Warren could not release his gaze from hers. He was locked in. Stung by a wasp.

She's reciting obscenities to him, Junie Moon thought, and her mind whirled back to her own dark night alongside the road. Lord God, Jesse, how come I stood there naked and let you say such things to me? She saw the same look on Gregory's face that had been on his—the stare without seeming to see.

"Warren!" she cried.

"Don't interfere, love," Gregory said without looking up. "This time we'll make it. Right, Warren? Now!"

With his powerful arms, Warren heaved himself out of his wheelchair and balanced on the armrests. He paused for a split second, and then with a mighty thrust he was up and on his thin legs. He swayed back once, like a dancer, and then pitched forward onto the floor.

"You see?" Gregory cried triumphantly to Junie Moon and Arthur. "You see, if he can stand like that, he can walk! Now again!"

"He did not stand, and you know it," Arthur said. His voice was unusually firm. Gregory looked at him, as if for the first time, and with interest.

"We will let Warren decide that," she said evenly.

"Indeed we will," Warren said, pulling himself back into

his wheelchair. He loved the fuss being made over him, especially now since he seemed to be back in Gregory's favor.

"He can't decide," Arthur said. Arthur did not understand the complexity of the scene before him. He knew only
that it was some form of cruelty, like many things that he
had seen at the institution. Little boys forced to drop their
pants to receive beatings for crimes they did not commit.
He himself locked in a broom closet for half a day. What
had he done? The offense escaped him now as it had then.
He tried to catch Junie Moon's eye. Why wasn't she helping
him with this mean woman? It was unlike her not to be putting in her two cents' worth. Junie Moon? Arthur felt faint.

For what seemed like an eternity, no one moved. Warren
with his face upturned, smiling at Gregory; Gregory, her
eyes hard, her mouth like stone; and Junie Moon, looking
past all of them, riveting her gaze on some minute speck of
plaster across the room, or so it seemed to Arthur. Arthur
thought: until I speak, nobody will speak ever again—we'll
stay frozen like this forever. Maybe I drank too much.
Maybe I'm going to have a seizure after all. Then quite suddenly, after he had run out of explanations to himself, he
realized, not without some shock, that he was in charge.

"We are going home now," he said at last.

Gregory jumped to her feet and put a hand on Arthur's
shoulder. "You can't go, darling! You just got here a while
ago." Was it panic he saw in her face? Whatever it was, it
was so ugly he almost felt sorry for her.

"Are you coming, Junie Moon?" he said.

Junie Moon tore her gaze away from the wall and looked
at him. "I suppose so," she said.

"You are coming too," Arthur said to Warren.

"Just a damned minute," Warren said, tears welling up again in his eyes. "You can't boss me around like this."

"Yes, I can," Arthur said, "from time to time."

Arthur took Junie Moon's arm and they walked down the long corridor, past the swimming pool, to the front door. The old-time music was still playing: *Pale moon shining, high above* . . . that same waltz. They waited by the door, neither of them looking at each other. In a few minutes they heard the whir of Warren's wheelchair coming toward them. His beard was wet from bawling, but he was ready to go.

Thirteen

Arthur's room was really a porch, since one end of it was screened. Warren had wanted to make it into a community room, suggesting that Arthur sleep on a cot next to the stove in the kitchen, but Arthur had won the battle by refusing to discuss the matter. Often at night as he lay in bed he could see the white flash of the owl's wings as the owl arranged himself in the banyan tree, and it reminded him of all the ghost movies he had ever seen with owls and bats and haunted houses. He pretended he was Laurence Olivier, lord of the manor, master of falcons and mastiffs and red-headed Irish mistresses, bent on some baronial hanky-panky. Most of Arthur's fantasies had a strong sexual story line. He dreamed about the act, the art and the vicissitudes of sex, mistaking it often for heroism or vanity—even love. Once in a while he still thought about Ramona. He remembered her great laugh as she stood at the chopping board in the kitchen of the state school waving her knife; teasing him with her wet mouth, nudging him with her rear end as he passed by. He played the scene again and again when she ripped the buttons off his pants, giving it a thousand different endings. And yet the scent of her was always too strong, the weight of her was always too heavy.

He awoke often at four in the morning, at a time when the winds died and the stillness was oppressive. At those times it was hard for him to think of sex. More often he thought: I am always sleeping among strangers.

He listened to the other two stirring in their rooms. Warren often chattered in his sleep and sometimes sang, and Junie Moon turned and twisted and flung herself about in the bed. At first he thought very little about Junie Moon in the night except that he was glad she was there. She was like an old shoe. An old aunt. An old homely sister. But she was changing. A little bit at a time she was getting less homely.

He had liked the feel of her belly when she had held his head in her lap at Gregory's and he had pretended to be asleep. But he still could not hold a sexual thought of her for very long in his mind. Instead he thought about what was happening to him. At four o'clock he worried about dying. It was always by drowning.

One night he got up and sat under the tree. He was having difficulty finding a point to his life, and that and his fear of dying made him feel dry and restless. He thought about running away, but he laughed wryly at himself because, of all the things he couldn't do, running away topped the list.

The awful weight of his leg with its dying nerves would permit him to go about as far as the drugstore. Maybe I could get a shot of adrenalin there, he thought, and make it another block. If a man can't run away, how can he become a respectable failure? Nevertheless, he could not sit around any longer. He was sick of charity. Tomorrow he would get a job. Having thought this, he noticed that the wind had begun to stir again, and he went inside and fell asleep.

The next morning he took a long and careful shower and put on some of the hair tonic Warren had given him. He did not know how to apply it, and as a result he looked like an old-time master of ceremonies with slicked-back, greasy hair. He put on a flowered sport shirt with short sleeves and a red and white striped tie. He had lost weight, so his trousers hung on the stems of his hips like they do on old men who are wasting away. He polished his shoes and cleaned his fingernails, but he had taken only a few steps out the front door when he was struck down by a seizure and lay for some minutes thrashing around in the weeds. When it was over, he crawled back into his room and lay down until he had recovered, and then he had to get cleaned up all over again. His frustration was so great that he was crying and his tears dribbled down his front, wrinkling his shirt. From her window, Junie Moon watched him in the final throes of his seizure and decided to do nothing about it since it was too late and since in the past Arthur had asked her not to bother. She heard his sobs and the water running in the bathroom and watched him go out the door again and down the path, his hair combed and his shirt tucked in. She thought: his goddamned heroics are going to make me bawl.

Arthur went back to the Western Union office where he

had worked previously and spoke with Sam, the man who had hired him.

"Well," Sam said, eyeing him from under his sun visor, "where have you been?"

Arthur decided to play it cavalier. "I've been to Florida," he said.

"Is that a fact?" Sam said. "And now I suppose you want your job back."

"That's right," Arthur said.

"No," Sam said, "that's wrong. You walked out of here without giving me any notice last time."

"I took sick," Arthur said, not meaning to.

"I thought you said you went to Florida." Sam knew that Arthur had been sick—a cop friend of his had found him on the street and had called the ambulance—but he felt like being mean.

"I was kidding about Florida," Arthur said. He knew that Sam was not going to hire him, but he couldn't seem to leave.

"You mean you were lying about Florida. I can't hire liars, Arthur. You know the company policy on that."

"I don't lie as a general rule," Arthur said.

"It's the exceptions to the rule that usually cause the worst trouble," said Sam, feeling a surge of good, warm honesty in his chest.

"I never caused you any trouble before," Arthur said. His hands were turning cold and he was rooted to the floor, unable to move.

"That's true, you never did," Sam said. "I'd be the first to admit that." He sat down at his old typewriter and carefully threaded in a message sheet. His smile was so warm that Arthur thought he was going to change his mind. "However,"

Sam said, "having once lied, I could never trust you again."
He began to type in a vigorous, rattle-bang way, and Arthur
knew he was not typing a message at all but trying to look
important and busy.

"I wouldn't need as much money as you paid me before,"
Arthur said, feeling sick at the sound of his own words,
wanting to beat himself for saying such a thing.

"What's that?" Sam cried over his own din. "I can't hear
you."

"Nothing."

"For Christssakes, you can speak up, can't you?"

For a wicked man, Arthur thought, Sam had such a
pleasant expression.

"How about if I worked the graveyard shift?" Arthur
asked. "It's always hard to get boys for that."

The terrible clatter of the machine stopped. "Look, Arthur, no is no. It's n-o." He hit a single key in time to his
words: "No, no, no, no, no!"

"All right, Sam." He was trying to move his leg, to get
the hell out, but nothing was happening. He was afraid he
was going to have to lie down and pull himself out on his
elbows.

"Take care of yourself now, Arthur. And have a good
time in Florida."

"You sonofabitch!" Arthur yelled. And the yelling tripped
the spring and his leg moved enough for him to make a step.

"Come back any time," Sam said pleasantly.

"You rotten bastard!" His muscles trembled like leaves
against the winter wind.

"The company policy about liars might change. Who
knows?" Sam said.

Go quick to the next place. Move now, move! Crying like a boob. Looking like a damned windmill going down the street. Move! Try the drugstore. Any place.

"I'm sorry," the pharmacist said. "I already have a boy."

"I'm not a boy!"

"I'm sorry about that too."

"Oh, shut up."

Move! Quick before it's too late.

"I used to have a porter, but I had to let him go."

"Why?"

"Because he ate up all the profits, that's why!"

"I don't eat much."

"That's what they all say."

It grew hotter and hotter and all the blood had drained from his hands and feet and had settled in his gut. I'm going to throw up all over the main street of the town, he thought.

"I don't know," Mario said, slicing off the head of a fat red snapper and tossing it into a pail. "Come back tomorrow. I'll ask the boss."

Lord God! a job.

Arthur thought he might never get home alive, but now that he had a reason to live, he didn't care. He thrashed up the path through the weeds and nasturtiums and rounded the house to the back yard, where he thought she would be. She was sitting under the tree reading last week's newspaper.

"I got a job," he yelled. "I got a job."

Then he fell into a heap at her feet, nearly fainting and coming as close to ecstasy as he had ever been. She took a lump of ice from her glass of lemonade and rubbed it on his forehead.

Mario did not know why he had told Arthur he would ask the boss, since he himself was the boss. But he was afraid that if he had said he didn't have a job Arthur would have dropped dead right there on the floor of his store, he had looked that terrible. It was true he could use somebody, but somebody strong to shovel ice and stack up the crates of fish.

Actually Mario could do all this himself, but what he wanted was someone to talk to. He missed the sound of another voice on the long summer afternoons. He missed someone to shout to on Fridays when the store was crowded. Well, he said to himself, what *did* the boss say? After a while, he answered his question. The boss says he doesn't know because there is something wrong with that young man. He might take a knife to the boss and throw the guts into the pail. Then later that afternoon, when he was closing up, Mario looked across the street and saw Arthur with the lady he had seen before—the one with the Mexican sombrero and the scarred face. To Mario it looked as if Arthur were pointing out the fish market to her. Oh my God, he thought to himself, he belongs in some way to her. *And then a great cauldron of soup came flying off the stove, nearly scalding me to death,* he heard his grandmother shout. Across the street, the lady with the sombrero patted Arthur on the shoulder and they turned and went back the way they had come. Lord, Lord, Mario said, he has come to show her where he is going to work. Ah well, he will be someone to talk to.

Fourteen

Arthur waited for Mario on the steps of the store. It was oppressively hot even at that hour of the morning, but he barely noticed. Although he had not slept more than five minutes the night before, he was as refreshed as a boy. He had crammed the fears as far back into his mind as he could, and he had used up the rest of the hair tonic.

Warren had spent most of the evening before making dire predictions: "He didn't say he would give you a job. He said he would ask the boss."

"That was only a formality."

"Besides, you'll come home stinking of fish."

"A man doesn't apologize for those kinds of smells," Arthur said loftily.

Junie Moon had to smile at him.

"I think it's romantic," she said. "Imagine! The fish you clean today slept last night in Chesapeake Bay."

"Cape Cod Bay!" Warren argued.

"How about an English sole, madam," Arthur said.

"I only eats Dover sole, dearie," she giggled, poking him in the ribs.

"Aye," said Arthur, "and only them tha's been run down by the steamer."

They were sitting under the tree, swatting at mosquitoes and eating brownies that Junie Moon had tried to make to celebrate Arthur's new job.

"You're going to spoil our idyllic arrangement by working," Warren said. "The next thing you know, the welfare ladies will be coming to teach *me* weaving or some other fascinating craft."

"They are doomed to failure," Junie Moon said.

Warren did not like others to say this. "You make terrible brownies," he snapped.

"I know it," she said.

"They are like poisonous stones."

"I would have to agree," she said.

"I can only think of one use for them," he said, taking one and firing it toward the hedge where Sidney Wyner usually hid to spy on them. They heard the brownie strike something—perhaps the stem of a plant—and then a faint rustling.

"You may have gotten him," Arthur said.

"Next time *you* make them," Junie Moon said.

"Thank you," Warren said, looking down his nose.

Sidney Wyner had been hit with the brownie, which he took to be a stone. It drove him indoors and he said to his wife, who was sorting through a large box of buttons, "The skinny one thinks he's got a job at the fish market. I'm going to fix his goose."

His wife looked up briefly and sighed. She was getting so tired of hearing about the people next door she could scream.

"Why don't you mind your own business, Sidney?" she said, letting the buttons slide through her fingers.

"That's exactly what I'm doing, Lil," he said, dialing the phone. "Hello, Mario," he said, "I've got something to tell you about that freak you hired." He then lowered his voice so that his wife could not hear what he was saying. His wife sighed again and examined the buttons in her hand. One of them came from the suit Sidney had worn to their wedding. "Oh God," she said aloud.

Mario had not liked listening to Sidney Wyner, knowing Sidney was meddlesome, but he had listened, much as one stares at a dirty postcard lying on the street. "He's a *what?*" Mario had said. Sidney had finally decided on the explicit type of perversion which afflicted Arthur.

"He's a sodomist," Sidney said.

"Is that a fact?" Mario said. It seemed to him that he had heard that word before, but he could not remember its exact meaning.

"I don't need to tell you," Sidney continued in an urgent whisper, "what hiring a guy like that might do to your business."

"Yeah," Mario said, slowly hanging up the phone.

Later that evening Mario tried to find the meaning of the word, but the only dictionary in his house was one his mother had used to teach herself English. It was printed in large letters and contained no reference to the word in question.

Mario took his time going to work that morning. He had a second cup of coffee, which was unusual for him, and sat for a while on the back steps of his house. Without being quite aware of it, he was beginning to be ruled by habits spawned from living alone, little rituals which would not have survived the demands of children or the scrutiny of a wife. For example, he entered the bed only on one side; he drank exactly two glasses of whiskey before dinner; he wore a different shirt each day and in an established order; and he kept only certain foods in his house—plain, unimaginative fare which gave him little pleasure. The summer had been too long, he thought, and he ached to feel a cool bite to the air. He was tired of the heat and the town and the stink of fish and always having to pick fish scales out of his hair and from under his fingernails. It had been months since he had spoken intimately with any woman, and much longer than that since he slept with one. He longed to be somewhere where people laughed and danced away the night until dawn. Instead, he finally got up and drove the long way to his store. From a block away he saw Arthur waiting, as he knew he would be. "You are a sodomist," Mario thought, still scratching through his mind for the definition. On the other hand, everybody knew that Sidney Wyner was a busybody and a liar. He must bear this in mind.

Despite the heat, Junie Moon had prepared a hot supper of mashed potatoes and beans and hot biscuits and pork chops—all the things she ever remembered Arthur saying he liked to eat. She had started cooking at four, and at six she was still going. Warren sat in the kitchen reading.

"This is nice," he said from time to time, smiling at her in such a beguiling way she found herself really liking him for the first time. "I like the way you hum when you work," he said. "My grandmother's cook in Boston used to do that."

"I do it to hide my fright," she said. "I haven't cooked in a coon's age."

"That's apparent, after tasting those brownies." He giggled wickedly at her over the top of his magazine.

"Okay, kiddo. I got the message." It was his fifteenth reference to her brownies in as many hours.

At a quarter to seven she had finished, but Arthur still had not come home.

"He probably stayed to tidy up," she said.

Warren grunted.

At seven-thirty the supper was growing quite cold. Warren was finished with the magazine and was hungry.

"We will wait a while longer," Junie Moon said, but when Arthur had not come by eight she fed Warren to keep him from nagging. They talked about other things, each pretending that Arthur would arrive momentarily. At ten-thirty, Junie Moon put on her sombrero.

"I'll just stroll down to the fish store and tell him that his supper is ready." She started out the door.

"He won't be there," Warren said.

"Oh, Warren," she said, "you'd take odds on the sun turning to ice."

It was dark and lonesome outside. People sat up on their porches talking, their voices muffled by the heavy summer leaves and by the hot, damp evening air. She kept as close to the curb as possible so that she would not be seen but would still be able to hear the talking. She loved the low hum of voices, even though it made her sad.

She felt very angry with Arthur. You dumb, stupid bastard, she said, as if he were standing in front of her. You pitiful, dumb bunny, you probably had a fit and fell into the crushed ice. Mario probably said to you: How are you, Arthur? and you said I am fine except I have a progressive neurological disease, and then Mario fired you before you were even hired. The more she thought about Arthur, the more enraged she became. She thought about the foolish way he combed his hair and how he wore striped ties with plaid shirts and humped along like a lame crab with his arms flapping like pincers. The trouble with you, Arthur, she thought, her face growing even redder over the scarred redness of it, the trouble with you is you're uncouth and you don't even know it! Junie Moon kicked a cardboard carton which lay in the gutter and it slithered over the sidewalk and came to rest in somebody's flower bed.

By the time she got to the post office where the town really began, she was so enraged with Arthur she was sick to her stomach. But almost at the same moment a tide coming from a completely different direction swept another thought into her mind: she remembered how Arthur had looked when he was telling her about the job. His smile, although she had not particularly noticed it then, had been as sweet as cream and his eyes had shimmered with excitement. It was at this point that Junie Moon broke into a fast lope, a pace she did not diminish until she got to the dark and empty fish market.

"Did you knock on the door?" Warren picked at his beard and scolded her with his tone of voice. "He might have been lying on the floor inside, for all you know."

"He wasn't inside."

"You're just assuming that, Junie Moon," he said. "Never send a woman to do a man's work."

"Right! Send a man!" She shot him a hard look. "I don't think he got the job."

"I tried to warn him," Warren said.

"You weren't warning him, you were threatening him."

"I was not!" Warren, sounding like a child, turned his wheelchair in short, angry arcs.

So they fought for a while, each blaming the other for what had happened to Arthur without even knowing what had happened. Neither one of them said what they were afraid of, that Arthur had gone and done something to himself.

At midnight Junie Moon went out again, this time to a telephone booth, where she looked up Mario's number. She dialed and it rang twenty-seven times before someone answered.

"I am coming to see you about Arthur," she said to the voice on the other end. And then she hung up.

Now the houses were dark. In one window a man in his bathrobe looked down into his garden, scratching his head

slowly as if he were planning his work for the next morning.
Behind him, Junie Moon saw a woman's hand, as though the
woman were lying in bed with her arm stretched into the
air. Maybe she was waiting for the man to come to bed.

She passed the hardware store where she had bought the
wagon and remembered Arthur's fury when he had first
seen their little house and the old-fashioned icebox. He had
been so angry he had almost cried. . . . "What will we haul
the ice in, I would like to know," he had said. Arthur had
beautiful eyes, Junie Moon thought, but they always tipped
his hand. You could tell exactly what he was feeling by one
glance into those eyes. "Damn you!" she cried out.

There was a light burning upstairs in Mario's house when
she got there. She rang the bell several times and listened to
the sounds he made before he came downstairs. He probably
thinks it's a robber, she thought, and is getting his gun.

"My name is Junie Moon," she said, standing in the darkness of the porch so he could get used to her face a little at a
time. "I came to ask you what happened to Arthur."

Mario stared at her and remembered that he had seen her
pass his shop and had seen her again with Arthur across the
street.

"Who is Arthur?" he said, knowing, but not knowing
how to tell her.

"He is a friend of mine. He and I and Warren live in the
little house under the banyan tree."

"Is that so?" he said, angry with himself for sounding so
dumb. He held out his hand, gesturing for her to come into
the house.

"You said you were going to give him a job," she said,

coming in but still keeping the hat close to her face. "Or at least it sounded to us as if you were."

He turned on a lamp and straightened a pillow on the couch and was suddenly aware of the mustiness of the room.

"Please sit down," he said. "You could take off your hat," he added softly. "It wouldn't bother me."

Junie Moon glared at him because she didn't believe him.

"What did you do with Arthur?" she said.

"I sent him away," Mario said, "because a man named Sidney Wyner told me he was a sex pervert. I didn't believe Sidney, but I sent Arthur away just the same." Mario's expression was so candid that Junie Moon could not be angry any more.

"Sidney Wyner lives next door to us," she said, "and he spends half his days and probably most of his nights hiding behind the hedge, peeping at us."

"I know," Mario said, laughing. "He's perfect for the part, especially in that filthy undershirt."

"You may think it's funny," she said, "but for Arthur it was probably the end of the world."

"I'm sorry," Mario said, running his hand quietly over his mustache.

"Then why did you do it? You must know by now that Sidney Wyner is a meddler."

"I don't know why," Mario said. The loyal way this strange woman was about Arthur made Mario catch his breath with sadness.

"He didn't come home," she said. "I cooked supper and we waited and waited and then I went to your store and he was nowhere to be found." The tension she had tried not to feel welled up in her and she began to cry.

"That was a bad thing for me to do," he said, offering her

his handkerchief. His feelings edged a breath beyond pity, but he could not explain them to himself. He patted her shoulder. "I'll help you find him."

Mario had a green panel truck with a pink fish painted on the side. As he went to the garage to get it, he was aware that his step was quicker than it had been in months. He smiled to himself. A man can think for only so long about fish, he thought. He helped Junie Moon onto the high front seat and they rattled off, Mario driving slowly and both of them looking along the dark tree-lined streets.

"Where do you think he might have gone?" Mario said.

"I don't know," she said. "He never had a special place—except the places he hated."

They drove all night, up one street and down the next, and when it began to get light they started on the country roads, going five miles out and coming back a different way.

"He's here somewhere," Junie Moon would say from time to time as if Arthur were a thimble she had misplaced. "He's so close I can almost smell him." And she would get Mario to stop the truck and she would get out and call Arthur's name. "God damn it, Arthur," she shouted once, "you come back here this minute!" As though he were a child hiding, but behind which rock?

At nine o'clock in the morning they went home. Warren was sitting red-eyed in the kitchen.

"Where the hell did you go?" he shouted at Junie Moon.

"We were looking for him," she said.

"Arthur always comes first around here, doesn't he? You never worry about me!"

"Oh, Warren, you weren't lost."

Warren glanced at Mario. "You would think Arthur was a hopeless case, the way she fawns over him."

"Ah," said Mario, trying not to smile.

"You would think," Warren continued, his eyes brimming with tears, "that Arthur were a wealthy little prince and Junie Moon were his English nanny—starched apron and all!"

Junie Moon made coffee and oatmeal for them. She patted Warren on the head and this calmed him down, but then he began to show off in front of Mario.

"She is a terrible cook," he said to Mario. "She makes brownies that crack your fillings and oatmeal with lumps as big as plums."

"Is that right?" Mario said.

"And she is a tyrant. There is no liberty in this house. She rules us both with an iron fist."

"Why don't you rebel?" Mario said. He was not really listening to Warren, preferring to watch Junie Moon at the stove. Despite her lankiness, she moved with a certain grace.

"They sting me with buckshot instead," Junie Moon said. "I'll die of an incipient anemia from a thousand tiny bleeding wounds."

Mario had never known anyone quite like these two—just when he thought he understood them, they switched and ran the other way, like a squirrel escaping a fast running dog. In his family the jokes had been broad and the relationships strong—either for or against, black or white. Only his grandmother with her mysteries and riddles and superstitions had been different. While the rest of them shouted and clumped through the house, she would sit on a grape box in the back yard, sorting through a silver box of beads and bracelets and rings with large yellow stones, all the while talking of the old days to the children—Mario was her favorite—who sat in the grass at her feet. Once Mario had worn the rings and bracelets to the dinner table, but his brothers had laughed so hard he had had to take them off. Ah, Grandma, he thought, his heart suddenly aching for her.

"I'd like you to come to my house," he said, startled by his own impulsiveness, which he did not understand.

Warren beamed. He was sure that Mario was charmed by him.

"That's very nice," Warren said. "When?"

"The thing about Warren," Junie Moon said, "is his shyness." She spooned out the oatmeal onto their plates. Mario smiled. The lumps *were* as big as plums.

After breakfast Junie Moon asked Mario to drop her off at the hospital. She had a feeling that Arthur would be there, probably dying, and ashamed to let her know. Mario wanted to come with her, but she was abrupt with him and slammed the door to his truck as she left, not saying goodbye.

The hospital that she had known so well was a strange place to her. To her surprise, she was now one of those who came in from the other world outside. The patients all looked thin and sick, even though she knew some felt better than others.

They had told her downstairs that Arthur was not there, but she went up anyway, not quite believing them. She looked into all the rooms except one, and she even went to the sun room they had hated so. It was Minnie's room she avoided. The television was playing in the sun room but no one was watching it except Vernon, the floor waxer, who had sat down to have a cigarette. He looked up and half nodded, not recognizing her in street clothes, but being unable to forget her scarred face.

"Hi," she said to him. "Did you see Arthur?"

"Who?" Vernon said, turning back to the television. He was watching a long-legged girl who was twirling a baton and doing a tap dance, all at the same time.

"Arthur. You know, he was a patient here when I was."

"They come and go," Vernon said, smiling as the girl leaned forward and crossed her feet over each other. All good dancers end with that step, he thought.

"Is that a fact?" Junie Moon said, but Vernon didn't hear.

At the nurses' station Miss Holt was counting out pills as she drank her morning coffee. When she saw Junie Moon she jumped up and coffee and pills and milk of magnesia spilled over everything.

"Well, I'll be damned," she shouted, giving Junie Moon a big hug. "It's Junie Moon. How are you all doing?"

"We've lost one," Junie Moon said. "I thought he might be here."

Miss Holt let her sit down in the nurses' station while she told her about Arthur. She got Junie Moon a cup of coffee and announced her presence to all the staff as they passed by.

"Miss Oxford took a long vacation after you three left," Miss Holt said. "We're all hoping that it will do her good."

"Are you sure Arthur didn't come here?" Junie Moon said.

Miss Holt shook her head. "He'll show up. By the way, did you see Minnie?"

"No," Junie Moon said. "I meant to but I never did.

Every day I meant to come to visit her, but for each day I didn't come, it got that much harder. Is she okay?"

"She's still alive, if that's what you mean."

As if she heard them talking, Minnie's high, childish voice was heard down the hall.

"Nurse! Nurse, you come here!"

"I'm coming, Minnie," Miss Holt called. Then she said to Junie Moon: "You go see what she wants. It would be a nice surprise to her."

"I don't think I can." Junie Moon felt a faint flutter inside herself and this frightened her. "Hospitals scare me."

"Are you kidding?" Miss Holt said. "After all you've been through?" She turned her back and started recounting the pills.

Junie Moon thought how close Miss Holt had been to them only such a short time ago. They had all lived together day and night and they had imagined that they had known all about her past, present, and future, and she had rubbed their backs and taken care of their most intimate needs, and now she was almost a stranger, turning away to count out the pills.

"I'll go see Minnie," Junie Moon said.

She walked as fast as she could to the room to get it over with before she changed her mind.

"Hello, Minnie."

"Lord God, it's Junie Moon!" Minnie said. "And I'm not even packed! Nurse!" she called. "Nurse! Vernon! Anybody! Come and help Minnie. Junie Moon has come to take her home."

Fifteen

The dog was not old but he acted old in that he tended to run sideways and for maybe ten steps at a time run on only three legs as though the fourth had been injured. He was a good, practical color— dark reddish brown—which enabled him to pass unobserved through the trees and shrubbery and, since he had never been given a bath by any human, to appear relatively clean. His coat was coarse and of medium length and he had a bristly muzzle and a good, strong, tapering tail. He could run like the wind.

The dog had had a number of masters. Some had discarded him and some *he* had left, but for the same reason: incompatibility. One of his early masters had insisted he learn to hunt deer, and for two seasons he was taken out into the hot underbrush, where he was encouraged to track the deer and return them for the man to shoot, but the dog did not enjoy this. He was half eaten alive by ticks and he found the man too intense and brutal (he was often hit with the butt of the rifle if he failed to track or to stay). One night he loped away from the man's house, glad to be rid of him.

Another place he left for quite different reasons. This time it was a lady who spent most of her time in her big, sweet-smelling kitchen, cooking and baking and reading romance magazines. He had ambled through her back yard one day and she had invited him in, offering him a plate of meat and vegetables. God knows he had been hungry that day, and this delighted the lady, whose chief pleasure, next to cooking and reading about romance, was watching others eat. He had not been there more than a week when she took to cooking special dishes for him—soup meat and oatmeal laced through with bacon fat and cheese rinds and fried steak tails. She gave him bowls of clotted cream with ice cream floating in it, and chocolate cake with marshmallow frosting. She fixed platters of soup with crackers on the top and little bowls of chicken giblets which she boiled first and then sautéed in butter. She called him three and sometimes four times a day to eat and at first he thought he had died and gone to heaven, he had never tasted such food. After a few days, however, he began to lose his appetite. This made the lady angry and she took to pouting and not looking at him, and the two of them walked stiff-legged around the kitchen, each hating the sight of the other. One day he went out, banging the screen door behind him, and both of them knew he would never come back.

He had been a tramp's dog for a little while, tailing a high-smelling old man out of town and spending about three weeks with him as he went north along the highway, but aside from seeing some new country, he hadn't enjoyed this too much. The tramp was a talky old man who went from one farmhouse to another, and oftentimes they were both set upon by big farm dogs and had to run for their lives.

He had almost stayed forever with a young boy whom he had come upon behind a barn, crying and kicking at the dirt. The boy had put his arms around the dog's neck and cried into his fur while the dog stood there staring at the mountains, waiting for the boy to finish. The boy fed him and brushed him and took him into the house, but his mother didn't like him and swatted at him when the boy was away at school. One day she chased him with a broom because he was sitting in her flower bed enjoying the morning sun. He had bitten her a little on the ankle and then had gone off.

So the dog went from one place to another and got to know pretty much within the first few minutes which people would like him; which people would like him and feed him; and which people would never feed him if hell were to freeze over.

One day during his travels he came across a man lying face down in a little rocky ravine about half a mile off the state highway and well hidden by trees. He circled the man slowly, his nose raised as if to discover more about him, and then he lifted his leg in a smart, military-type salute and peed against the side of an oak tree, never taking his eye off the man. When this did not stir the man, the dog stiffened his hind legs and kicked out a great cloud of leaves, making low throaty noises as he did. The man did not respond, and the dog walked away, pretending to do something else but all the while listening for a telltale movement on the part of the man. The sun rose high in the sky and a handful of flies came and rested on the back of the man's neck, but he made no move. The dog found himself a spot of shade under an elderberry bush. He could watch the man even with his eyes rolled halfway back in their sockets. Although a buzzard circled overhead, the dog stayed and watched, so convinced was he that eventually the man would stir.

The ambulance pulled up in front of the house and out jumped a uniformed lady whose big breasts strained the buttons of her strict jacket, and two uniformed men. Sidney Wyner hissed at his wife to come and look, but she was picking snapdragons and pretended she could not hear him.

The attendants opened the back door and removed a stretcher, a kind that Sidney had never seen before. Suspended from poles over it were various bottles which seemed to be carrying liquids in and out of the patient's body. Whoever the patient was, it was hard to tell, for a gray blanket came within an inch of totally obscuring its face. The men stood holding the stretcher while the woman attendant bent over the patient, and the four of them waited while Junie Moon got out and led the way up the path to the house.

Warren was sitting under the tree and Junie Moon barely looked at him.

"I've got Minnie here with me," she said to Warren, "and if you say a word about it, I will beat you to death with the poker." And with that the litter-bearers advanced, the uniformed woman bringing up the rear as though she might be their sergeant major.

Then Minnie's voice, thin and persuasive, came from under the blanket.

"Set me down out here," she said.

The men were doubtful. They had been instructed to deliver her to some safer ground, but the woman attendant convinced them it would be all right to put Minnie down on an old cot under the tree.

"She'll manage," she said to the two men, indicating Junie Moon. And away they went.

"I never have seen a tree like this one in all my days," Minnie said. "It seems to go on and on forever." Then she rolled over on her side. "Why, it's Warren. How are you, Warren?"

"Just peachy," Warren said.

"That's good," she said. "I haven't been peachy in a long while. I've been tired, and sore . . . and restive, but not peachy for longer than I care to remember. Did Junie Moon tell you that I've come to stay? Where is that other nice man? The one with fits?"

"He went looking for a job," Junie Moon said quickly.

"Humph," said Warren.

"I want to wish him a lot of luck," Minnie said. "When he comes back to our little place, you must remind me to do that."

From next door Sidney Wyner's wife, who was sick to death of her husband's spying on the neighbors, happened to glance through the hedge and see Minnie lying on the cot under the banyan tree. She was so startled by what she saw that she called to her husband.

"That new one," said Mrs. Wyner, "is black!"

"They're *all* black as far as I'm concerned," Sidney said.

She patted his hand and smiled at him for the first time in weeks and he carried her snapdragons into the house.

At 1:45 in the afternoon the sun was blazing hot and nothing stirred. The air was heavy with the smell of dry grass and dry seeds and earth which had gone too long without rain. Heat crystals seemed to fill the air, distorting things in the distance, like the view through a smoked windowpane. The dog grew restless under the elderberry bush, partly because of the heat and partly because the project in which he had become involved was not working out the way he had expected. The man still had not moved. Being a modern dog, he could have walked away and gone on to other adventures, but something out of his ancient past made him linger. He paced for a while, irritated with his inner compulsion, wanting a drink, hating the heat, which reminded him of his deer-hunting master, being willing to settle even for the lady who fed him too much, wishing the young boy had overpowered his mother and kept him. He stayed. After a while he sat between the man and the sun so that his own shadow was cast over the man's head. The dog sat there and waited.

"Where is she going to sleep?" Warren hissed.

"Don't worry," Junie Moon said. "Go in and make us some nice cool lemonade and a plate of brownies."

Warren was so angry with her that he did exactly as he was told.

"I knew you'd come and get me," Minnie said. "Everybody at the hospital said I was a liar. They said, 'Old Minnie is lying again, telling us that Junie Moon is coming to get her.' I guess I fooled them. Lordy, I wish you had come right in the middle of Grand Rounds and carried me away from under their noses." She imitated the resident's nasal voice: " 'How are you feeling today, Minnie? That's good.' Never waits for an answer, never listens if he gets one. And just to think I'm breathing real air out under a tree for the first time in two years. Oh, Junie Moon, I'll give up my grave to you if you ever find you need one." She lay back and tears streamed down her cheeks.

"Don't cry," Junie Moon said.

"It's all right," Minnie said. "This isn't mourning crying or hurt crying. It's relief crying. It's such a relief to lie here and cry and look up into that old tree." Minnie sighed, her frail hand falling over her eyes as if she were rummaging through the past. Junie Moon went into the kitchen to help Warren.

"Isn't it enough," he snapped, "that Arthur is gone, but you have to add Minnie to our worries."

"I didn't know you had any worries," Junie Moon said. She felt like having a good fight with Warren. He could yell and scream and make a fight worthwhile, enabling a person to get rid of a lot of bile, but she thought it might scare Minnie. "She won't stay long. You'll see."

"That's what they said at the hospital, that she wouldn't live from one day to the next."

"It's mean, what you're saying."

"Nobody asks me anything. They just go their merry way and then it's good old Warren, he'll make the lemonade, he'll make the brownies."

"I never called you good old Warren in my life," Junie Moon said. She must stop herself now, she thought, because the fight was about to start, little of it having to do with Minnie.

"I'm sorry," she said, forcing herself to pat his shoulder. She knew he liked to be touched and hugged, even by her, and this was the quickest way she had found to placate him.

"I hear those sweet voices of yours coming from inside the house," Minnie called. "It's such a comfort to hear that sound again."

Even Warren had to smile. But he was soon petulant again. "I'm going to look for Arthur. I can't sit around here making a tea party when God knows what's happened to him." He held his head in his cocky way as he wheeled out the door, but Junie Moon knew, despite this, that Warren was worried. She took Minnie a glass of lemonade and a cooling cloth for her forehead.

"Warren shouldn't wheel around in the heat," Minnie said. "He's liable to get a sun stroke. When you lie in bed as much as I do, you see how much pointless running around people do. Like chickens with their heads cut off. By the way, did you ever see a chicken beheaded?"

"That's one thing I missed," Junie Moon said.

Minnie turned so she could get a better view of Junie Moon. "My grandma kept a little flock of hens and every once in a while she'd decide one of them was getting too old and had to go into the pot. She had a chopping block out by the barn and a hatchet which she used to keep filed as sharp as a razor. She said those old hens could smell when a killing was coming. The minute she came into the pen, those hens knew she hadn't come to pass the time of day. They would start to look queer and nervous and make little sounds like they were muttering under their breath and they would walk faster and faster in all directions. 'Stand still, you damned old fools,' she would yell at them, and this would set them off even more. And the one she was after would know it too and try to find a place to hide in the broad daylight. But Grandma would catch her at last and sit down with the hen in her lap and I would say, 'Hurry up and get it over with!' After a while she would stroll over to the chopping block and all the other hens would line up to watch and *whack* it was finally done. Then that beheaded old hen would get up off the block and with blood spurting all over the place would run around the yard. I tell you, she ran into me the first time I watched and I let out a scream you could hear for ten miles. How Grandma laughed."

"Some joke," said Junie Moon.

"Which only goes to show you," Minnie said, "how much unnecessary running around there is in this world."

The grass was like barbs against his face—this was the first thing he was aware of—as though a giant hand were pressing up from under the earth, crushing his skin. His mind was lost in that it would not tell him where he was or how he got there, and he was afraid that if he opened his eyes before he found out, he would be doomed and never know. Things floated piecemeal in his mind: a leg he was unable to move; a typewriter with all the keys caught in a bunch; a woman's voice calling his name. Then the smell of fish acted as the key which brought everything together. He opened one eye and saw a big red dog sitting a few feet away. He thought: the dog is here to kill me. I came to just long enough to observe my own death. He closed his eye.

Warren telephoned Gregory and told her that Arthur was lost.

Her voice icy, "Who is Arthur?" she said. She had lost interest in all of them, but she let Warren borrow her car and chauffeur, and for the next five hours they searched the streets. Everyone in town who was outside that day saw them, they drove so slowly. From time to time Warren was so carried away with his own image that he forgot why he had come, and at last the chauffeur suggested they call it a day, mainly because they had run out of streets.

"If you think so," Warren said, using a lofty English accent.

By 3:30 Minnie had told her last story and fallen asleep and awakened again to stare up through the branches of the tree. Junie Moon was in the kitchen washing the dishes, but she could see Minnie through the window. Coming home had been only partly Junie Moon and Minnie's idea. The resident had been in on it. This was the resident that Junie Moon liked and he had taken her aside and told her that Minnie talked of them day and night and had almost worn herself out.

"It's not that she really wants to live with you," the resident had said. "It's the fact that she's told all the other patients that you are coming to get her."

"But she can't stay with us," Junie Moon said. "We live in a chicken pen under a tree that's as big as a circus tent, and we're ankle deep in mildew."

"Just for a few hours," said the resident. "Then I will come and get her."

"Why would you do that?" Junie Moon curbed the impulse to hug him.

The resident held her face between his hands. "Because I'm an emotional subversive," he said.

So at four o'clock, as he said he would, the resident came with the ambulance and pretended to scold Minnie for running away from the hospital. Minnie, who had already begun to worry about what would happen to her when night came and there was no nurse, managed a grin and invited him to sit down and have a glass of lemonade. She acted just as though she had lived in the little house with Junie Moon and Warren and Arthur for years, which was just as well, for now she could go back and tell the other patients all about life under the tree, and tell them, furthermore, that the resident had kidnapped her and brought her back to the hospital against her will.

On his way home from his store, Mario stopped at their house, bringing a big basket with him. In it were shrimp, some Dover sole, a loaf of Portuguese bread, and half a gallon of strong red wine.

"Hey, Junie Moon," he cried, banging at the back door. "Come and let me in."

Sidney Wyner was just sitting down to his own supper next door, but he interrupted it to see what was going on. As he left the table, his wife called to him: "It's more of their shenanigans, you can bet."

Sidney grinned and licked his lips. It pleased him that after all this time his wife was finally aware of the disgraceful activities next door.

"I brought the best in town," Mario called. He put the

basket in the sink and began to prepare the fish while Junie Moon watched. It was as though they were old friends—or lovers—her watching him without saying anything.

"He didn't come yet? He will." He threw a handful of herbs into a pot and stewed them up with the shrimp and he poured out the wine in two jelly glasses. "Cin-cin," he said. He had not eaten this well in months.

When Warren came home, Mario fussed over him, so much so that Warren enlarged upon his account of the afternoon—he had driven in a Rolls-Royce and had been attended by a coachman. Mario appeared to believe him, and Junie Moon smiled at the two of them. If the liar has a listener, she thought, it is the liar who is really fooled.

After they had eaten, they sat under the tree. The wind blew, but it was a hot, irritating wind which brought no relief from the heat.

Warren glanced from time to time down the street as though Arthur might come along at any minute. He was angry for not having found Arthur, thinking that he would have been a hero if he had, at least in the eyes of Junie Moon.

"He has gone away to another state," Warren said.

"Oh, for pity's sake," Junie Moon said, fanning herself with a banyan leaf.

Mario gazed up at the sky. He wished he knew how to comfort these two. He had cooked the fish and told them stories about what had gone on at the store that day . . . he had even done a little dance step as he had served the food, but neither of them had smiled or even listened well for that matter.

It was as though they were all waiting in a depot where the tracks had been torn up.

◆ Sixteen

The dog stayed and finally he saw the man's eyelid flicker. He grunted and shifted in the sun: it would not be long now before something happened.

Arthur raised his head a few inches, but the effort exhausted him and he rested it again, but this time with his eyes open, on the dog. The dog's wet red mouth was like an internal organ, throbbing and intimate. Dogs do not perspire, he thought. If they stink, it is because they have rolled in something or they have a rotten tooth, and no popular deodorant could possibly touch their problem. No man-sized, roll-on, nothing-touches-you-but-the-spray will cure a doggie of B.O.

Across the field came the thin sound of traffic from the highway. At first he thought it was the whir of insects—

long, careening sounds ending on high notes—but then he decided it was the screech of tires on a poorly banked curve.

Which reminded him that only once he had driven a car. A truck, really, which he had kicked into gear accidentally at the state school. It had raced off down the dirt road with only him in the cab. Trees flying by like in an old-time movie. He had gotten behind the wheel and steered the thing, and he was as close to heaven as he would ever be and still be alive, for the first time in years moving without jerking or flailing. In forty-three seconds he had learned to drive, had taken his first trip, gone over his first bump, turned his first corner, torn up his first potato patch, broken his first speed limit, and had his first accident. No one could ever say to him, "You can't hit the broad side of a barn." He had.

The dog cocked his head to one side. Now that the man had finally showed signs of life, perhaps there would be an end to the heat.

There was no doubt about the fact that he would have to try to get up, Arthur thought. He had no idea how long he had been there or if this mattered. The fish store was now clear in his mind, with Mario turning him away. He remembered that then he had felt a great surge of anger, strong enough to propel any number of violent reactions: murder, tears, a seizure, a prolonged silence, but he had stood there like a senseless fool—retardate—his tongue paralyzed with disappointment, his body trembling, a dead giveaway.

He had listened once through a door to a lady at the state school speaking to a group of visitors. "We attempt to help the retardate realize his potential," she had said. What does retardate mean, dummy? That's what it means: dummy!

Where were you when they gave out the brains? Upstairs in the shower, playing with myself!

"Come here, dog."

The dog narrowed his eyes.

Arthur would first have to pull his leg up under him and push up with his arms. The entire process of getting up off the ground would have to be taken apart, analyzed, weighed, and measured. His stomach rocked, leaving him in a cold sweat. He would count backwards from fifty and by then his stomach would settle and he could approach the problem.

Ramona, you left me standing there with my pants around my ankles. That was not helping me to realize my potential.

A trembling muscle dragged up his leg but would not hold it there and he fell down again, this time crushing dried burs against his mouth. The pulse that beat in his ears was like a soft-shoe rhythm. Dum-de-dum-de-dum-de-dum-de-dum. Tell me that you love me—tell me that you love me—tell me that you love me, Junie Moon, waa-waa. Tell me that you love me, tell me that you'll kiss me, tell me that you miss me, Junie Moon, waa-waa.

He had not made it counting to zero backwards, so he threw up and for a while lay there gagging, and then he thought: I am going to die. I will choke in my own juice with no one but this stupid dog watching. It was only then that he made the supreme effort and was able to get to his knees.

"Help! Help me!" On all fours like a baying dog. The effort and the heat and his terrible fear sent his heart spinning as though the pulse were now one continuous roar, punctuated at microscopic intervals. The soft shoe was like a runaway phonograph record. Tell-me-that-you-love-me-Junie-moon-waa-waa, tellmethatyoulovemejuniemoon,waa-waa!

He grabbed the scruff of the dog's neck and pulled himself erect. The dog growled but did not bite him. He took twenty-two steps to a big tree and fell into the shade. The dog lay nearby, glad to be out of the sun.

I will have a plate of fried brains with a side order of plaques. That's right, plaques for good behavior, plaques for bravery, and a special plaque to commemorate my bygone days.

And then he wept. He wept because he could no longer pretend to be brave, and because it was like what Warren, or was it Guiles, had said: that you wept when there was no place left to go. He brayed and bawled and kicked the ground, and screamed every swear word he had ever heard, and then he called the dog names and piled abuse on him as though he knew him. The dog flattened his ears as though it were raining and averted his eyes until Arthur stopped screaming. Then the dog got up and started off.

"You come back here," Arthur screamed. The dog turned slowly and came back, and then Arthur's tears were like those of a silly girl who has just been kissed.

After a while he got up and started toward the highway, the dog trotting behind.

Seventeen

Arthur did not come home that day or the day after that. Junie Moon went to all the places she remembered him having talked about, including the state school. Mario drove her there and they pretended they had a little boy they wanted to put away in the school and the officials let them look around. She even went out into the tomato patch where Arthur said he used to work with a boy named Gembie, and while they were there Junie Moon wondered if the girl who dried her hair on the porch would remember Arthur now. Had he really seen the North Pole when he looked up her dress? Junie Moon felt a sharp nostalgia for Arthur which she had not expected, since she would only admit to herself that she was executing a friendly duty by looking for him. She had never known anything about the past lives of the men she had cared about and so this journey was like being taken home to meet the in-laws.

"I wonder which of those buildings he slept in?" she said.

"It's as big as a city," Mario said. "It would be hard to tell." He looked at her out of the side of his eye, and it dawned on him then that the strange irritability he was feeling all morning might be jealousy. "Ho!" he shouted aloud, jolted by his sudden awareness.

She gave him her mock-mean look. "Ho happens to be my word," she said.

The weather had changed that morning, a sharp wind bringing the first taste of fall. The state school was bleak and faded, and as they crossed the grounds they pressed their shoulders close together, each seeking the warmth of the other.

"Arthur is important to you, eh?" he said, trying to sound casual.

"You bet," she said. "I'm after his money."

"Ahhhh." What he had wanted to ask was: is he your person? But he hadn't the nerve. Suppose her answer were yes. Did they sleep together? Suppose her answer were no. How could anyone sleep with a woman who had such a face and had stumps for hands. When the moon shone in the window through the trees, what then? *Then the cauldron crashed from the stove, pouring a fountain of hot soup like lava from Mount Etna. Can you guess the sin I was punished for?* He remembered his grandmother's face as she waved her scalded arm under their noses. She was always merry about it. Why? He stole a look at Junie Moon. The wind had blown up the edges of her sombrero, leaving her face exposed in the raw cold air. She looked far from merry, and he could only think of masks he had seen once in a primitive museum. And yet she had stirred him and there would be no simple way out. Old bachelor—you thought you'd be so smart.

"Let's go eat something," he said, finding it impossible to say anything more personal.

They drove back along the highway and about three miles down the road Junie Moon saw them. They were heading in the same direction, toward town, walking in the dry stubble beside the road, the man in front and the dog bringing up the rear.

"My God," Junie Moon said, "it's Arthur."

"I didn't know he had a dog," Mario said, slowing down the truck.

"He doesn't," said Junie Moon, rolling down the window.

"It looks like a dog to me," Mario said, irritable again.

"That only goes to show you that you see what you want to see," she snapped.

He thought: all of her is directed toward a shambling man and a flea-bitten dog. She's a monster, and I should forget it.

The trouble was, he was having difficulty remembering it.

Arthur did not notice them immediately when they pulled alongside. Mario kept pace with him, and watching him walk was like watching a bird with a broken wing trying to get off the ground. He was dragging one leg as though all the muscles in it had died. He would heave it up and swing it around as if it were hanging by a string from his belt, and then he would half-hop half-jump on it, knowing the leg would not support him for more than a split second. His arm on that side was drawn close to his body, with the fist turned in like that of an infant, while the other hand circled the air in front of him as if it were searching for something stable to cling to.

"Arthur!"

He stopped abruptly and looked at her, but he could not make sense of what he saw: Junie Moon in Mario's truck with the fish painted on the side. He thought he was dreaming, and began his painful walk again, riveting his eyes on a black tree up the road.

"Arthur, it's me!"

If he could make it to the tree, he would sleep awhile and then go on. However, if he could not make it to the tree, he would die and lie in the ditch getting speckled with road oil until some lazy highway patrolman saw him rotting there. Move out the queen's pawn. Move it, move it, and the devil with it! Queen's pawn to queen's pawn four. You could fool the piper with that baby move. Peter piper packed a pound of pickle paper. Please, dear Arthur, keep your mind on the game.

To counter: move the black bishop one and one half squares southwest. Silly. The black bishop is a Moor and would run off the map going southwest.

"Arthur, it's Junie Moon. Your oldest friend!"

Tell me that you love me, Junie Moon, waa-waa.

"You get into this truck. Mario didn't mean to do what he did."

"Ho!" Arthur screamed.

" 'Ho' happens to be your word," Mario said, grinning senselessly at her.

"You shut up," Junie Moon yelled at him.

Arthur turned his back as he usually did when he was angry or upset.

"Come home, do you hear?" Junie Moon shouted.

Mario stopped the truck and the dog walked over on stiff, suspicious legs and peed on the front tire.

"Yaaa," Mario shouted at him, and the dog flattened his ears and went to sit beside Arthur.

"You are wasting your breath talking to either of them," Mario said. And to his surprise Junie Moon said: "You're right. Let's go home."

"Are you sure?" he said.

"Yes. He will take his sweet time, but he will come home now."

"How do you know?"

She smiled. "Because he was already on the way. We didn't find him at all."

Arthur did not come home that night, although Junie Moon and Mario and Warren waited for him out under the tree until two o'clock in the morning.

"If you saw him," Warren said, "why didn't you bring him home?"

"You have asked me that question twenty times," she said, pulling on an old sweater of Arthur's around her shoulders.

"He wouldn't look at us," Mario said.

"If *you* had handled it," Warren said to Mario, "you would have had him home." Warren had developed a crush on Mario and had spent the entire evening flattering him and feeding him platter after platter of brownies. "You would have picked him up and set him gently into the truck. Right, Mario?" Warren particularly admired the fine hard muscles that rippled over Mario's forearms, and his small but undoubtedly very powerful hands. "I could tell that Mario would be quite persuasive if he put his mind to it," Warren continued, and Junie Moon let out a loud laugh. "Perhaps we're keeping you up?" he said to her. He wished she would go to bed and leave him alone with Mario.

"It is Arthur who is keeping us up," Mario said.

He had never been flattered by a man before and it amused him. In his family, men fought and yelled and to show affection knocked each other's biceps.

"You liked Arthur?" Mario said.

"Just what do you mean by that?" Warren said, narrowing his eyes.

Mario laughed. "Nothing bad. A friend, perhaps?"

"Well . . ." Warren had never had a friend. He had had lovers. And girlfriends who were more like sisters. And older women who petted him. And women like Gregory who bought him for experimental purposes. But he had no friends. "Of course he was my friend," he said cheerily. He would not let this nice fisherman in on any of his dark or forlorn thoughts. It might depress him.

"I like him," he continued, "despite the fact that he has a very difficult personality. He isn't friendly and direct like you."

"Ahhhh," said Junie Moon, slapping at a mosquito.

"He is given to silent spells and dark moods," Warren said, "so in order to be his friend you have to put up with a lot."

"Look who's talking," Junie Moon said.

"He is as rigid as a bedboard," Warren said, ignoring her remarks. "He thinks that welfare is a sin and that laughter is only for certain holidays."

"Which holidays?" Mario said, smiling.

"I don't know because we have yet to celebrate one," Warren said.

Of course he was right in a way, Junie Moon thought. Arthur's dark, pensive ways were so clear in her mind that she felt the tears beginning to form. He was such a stubborn ass, running away and then not getting into the truck. Damn him! And yet that made the form of him, outlined his particular predictability.

"He gets up at six o'clock every morning," Warren went on. "Did you know that? He said it was a hangover from living at the state school, but I know better. He really thinks that anyone who stays in bed past 6 A.M. is headed for hell. God Almighty, he wakes us both up with his stomping around before it was light outside. Isn't that true, Junie Moon?"

"I am always awake anyway," she said. But she thought: for Arthur, the night is full of terrors and he is always glad when it is over.

"He had a very deprived childhood," Warren said, "which probably explains it all."

"And you didn't, I suppose?" Junie Moon said.

"Of course not," Warren said. "I had Guiles during my formative years, and then my grandmother, who happened to be a biochemist. Did you know that?" he said to Mario.

"Of course he didn't know that," Junie Moon said. "He just met you."

"And my mother was a very beautiful woman, so I am told. There are certain advantages in having a mother you have never seen, especially if she was beautiful and a golden legend."

"There is always a bit of truth in what you say," Junie Moon said.

Mario went home after a while, saying he would come with rainbow trout for breakfast.

Warren went to bed, and for a long time, until almost dawn, Junie Moon sat under the banyan tree trying to arrange her feelings in a more acceptable design. She had thought that life in the little house would be more pesky than anything else and that they would spend their time talking about their aches and pains and plotting a course with the welfare agency, but there had been very little of this, and she felt instead that she was nailed to a flatcar which was tearing across a dark desert.

It was not until she heard the sound of the owl's wings that she knew she was afraid. "You were supposed to bring us luck," she called up to the owl. He acknowledged this by sending down a shower of tiny bones and fur. He had caught and killed a blind, shrieking mole, and had settled down for his predawn snack.

"You are a fake and a phony," she said to the owl, "representing yourself as mystical and wise and then appearing as a plain old greedy bird." She closed her eyes, but all the half-finished things of her life would not permit her to sleep. There was Jesse who was still free as a bird and probably pouring acid over other women; and there was her mother and daddy, gone without telling her, to live on a beach in the white sun; and there was this house that needed a good scrub; and there was Arthur, who she now admitted troubled her the most, who was gone almost before he came, mourned before he died; and almost, but not quite loved.

As soon as she fell asleep, sitting under the tree, Arthur came home. He dragged one foot after the other, walking like a man in a painful trance. He stood looking at Junie Moon for a moment before he went into the house. The screen door closed, and the dog, who had been following only a few steps behind, opened the door with a curved paw and went inside too.

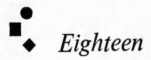

Eighteen

The smell of frying fish woke the dog and he shook himself and walked carefully into the kitchen. He had not slept enough, but he was thirsty and half starved and he had to find out in a hurry if anyone in this house would feed him. Otherwise he would go on his way.

Mario was frying the fish in a big iron skillet and Junie Moon and Warren were sitting facing each other across the kitchen table.

"He's a friend of Arthur's," she explained about the dog. "He slept on the bed next to Arthur, with his head on the pillow."

"How do you know?" Mario said sharply. Jealousy made his hand tremble.

"Because I looked in and saw them," she said. "That dog was smack in the middle of the bed and there was hardly any room for Arthur." She laughed. "I put a blanket over Arthur, but I couldn't cover one without the other."

The dog walked lightly across the linoleum as if he were stealing something, and rested his head on Junie Moon's lap.

"He likes you," Warren said.

"No, he doesn't," Junie Moon said. "He's hungry and thirsty and a damned con artist, that's all."

"My grandmother had two Pekingese who sat side by side in a highchair for the evening meal," Warren said. "They were served along with everyone else."

Junie Moon got up and fixed the dog some breakfast: a can of corned beef hash with cornflakes topped off with a fried rainbow trout. She filled the mop pail with water and put that and the pan of food out under the banyan tree. The dog followed after her, wagging his tail slowly from side to side.

"You two should take Arthur on a vacation," Mario said abruptly when Junie Moon came back into the house. Warren giggled, not daring to believe what he heard.

"We cannot afford a vacation," Junie Moon said.

But Mario had thought it all out. He had not slept when he went home. Instead he paced through his large, empty house, wishing for the sound of voices. Several times before in his life he had regretted that he had not married and filled his house. His brothers and their fat wives chided him until it had become a habit. Mario-hey-kid-when-you-gonna-get-married? How come, they said, he stayed in that dark old house. Why not sell it and get a little modern split-level, something a modern girl would like. Come on, Mario, catch up with the times. Often on Sundays he would visit one or the other of them in their modern houses, eating too much of the heavy food prepared in their modern kitchens, sitting afterwards in the living rooms that were too neat and too small for comfort. The little houses were all right, he thought, but there was no place to go after a big meal, no porch with a hammock. And the back yards were paved and without trees.

His house got bigger and emptier as the years passed. His grandmother, before she died, had pulled his head close to her own and whispered, "Get yourself a woman, Mario, before your legs grow thin and tired." Even on the hottest day his house seemed cold. A woman came to clean and to put things straight, but nothing shone, and, except for his room, the house smelled sour and unused. He had never thought of himself as remaining unmarried. And when he was ready, he thought, he would be able to find a pretty girl with dark eyes who would wrap herself around him on cold winter nights and give him all the children he wanted. When I am ready, he would say to his brothers and their wives. You will see, when I am ready. But the girl with the dark eyes was nowhere, and he did not love her any more, and would not, even if she were real. Because now there was this long-legged woman who wore a Mexican sombrero to hide her terrible face. What would you say to that, Grandmother? This silly, unfathomable creature who runs instead of walks, always a little sideways, making me laugh with her sly jokes.

By the time dawn came, he was beginning to know something above love, but since he could not bend it to fit his dream or think of a speech that his brothers would listen to without their glancing sideways at their fat wives, he decided on another plan. He would send Junie Moon and Arthur and Warren off on a vacation. Out of his hair. Out of his house.

"I have not been on a vacation in years," Warren said, tapping his finger nervously on the tabletop. He was trying to contain himself so he would not spoil it.

"You can go in my truck," Mario said, "and I will loan you the money."

"No," Junie Moon said, "that won't work." There was a sadness in her voice which even Warren noticed.

"It would do Arthur a world of good," Warren said hopefully.

"I doubt it," said Junie Moon.

"Why don't we ask Arthur," Mario said.

"Oh no, no, no," Warren said. "He would never go in a million years after what you did to him. And in your truck! I can hear him ranting and raving now."

"Is that so?" Arthur was standing in the doorway, his hair tousled from sleep. "I see everyone is deciding my life for me—as usual. Where is the dog?"

"I gave him breakfast in the yard," Junie Moon said.

"I want to apologize," Mario began.

"I don't want you to," Arthur said. "It would make me sick and I'm too hungry to be sick."

Mario stood holding a plate of trout in his hand, not knowing what to do with it.

Then Arthur took them all off the hook. "I think the vacation is a fine idea," he said. "I don't even care if you pay for it. But one thing."

"What, what?" Warren was almost beside himself.

"The dog comes too," Arthur said.

"Will you come?" Junie Moon said to Mario.

"No," Mario said quickly. And he put the plate of fish on the table in front of Arthur.

Mario fixed a bed in the back of the truck for Arthur which the dog promptly got into. He sewed mitts for Junie Moon's damaged hands so that she could drive. He went to his house, where he boiled eggs and put canned things from his cellar into a box with the eggs. He packed these and a gallon can of water and a box of matches and twenty-five feet of hemp rope with an assortment of road maps and two tins of hard candy.

"You would think we were going on a safari," Arthur said.

When they weren't looking, Mario put a short-handled shovel into the truck and a hatchet and a frying pan. He made strong, neat packages of everything, and while he was doing it he wanted to go with them so badly he could taste it.

They left at five o'clock the next morning. Mario put them into his truck as if they were his life—his jewels, his reputation. In the glove box he put an envelope with $900— pinned it to the first map they were bound to use. He hoped that when they got out on the highway the truck wouldn't still stink of fish.

Warren sat on the front seat with the window open. He sang a dreary collection of camp songs and commented on this and that and that and this until they wanted to swat him. But they could not make him angry.

Arthur lay on the bed in the back with the dog beside him. The dog swayed and looked a little queasy from the cornering and turning. Arthur felt as though he had been fished from a cold river and put into a box behind the stove—only the box was moving and there were the voices of a man and a woman lulling him, making him believe that he had a family or at least some small root which would help him to know the earth. Tell me that you love me, Junie Moon, waa-waa. He remembered the sun beating on him and the taste of dry grass and he wondered then why he had run off and if she had even worried.

Warren had made the plans. The sea, he said, was better than the mountains at this time of year. The best people would be there. It would be square to go any place else. They had not even tried to oppose him.

"They say," Warren said, "that the jet set will be going to Alaska next. It's supposed to be way out, what with the glaciers and the pure, pure snow."

"The jet set," said Junie Moon, "would have difficulty telling the pure, pure snow from the back of their hands."

"Why are you always so cynical?" Warren said. "You sound like a sideways Puritan."

She laughed. "It's better than being mean." But she stole a glance at him, and his sweet face, so full of the holiday, melted her a bit.

"You're right," she said. "I'm beginning to sound like a clever old maid. I think it has something to do with sex—or the lack of it."

With this, Junie Moon felt Arthur's breath behind her ear from the bed of the truck. He always came alive when sex was mentioned, and she pushed him away like she always did—pesky fly, go lie down.

He thought: It's nice to be pushed back by a woman who doesn't mean it, and he stretched out and took a playful poke at the dog. The dog, who was growing fond of Arthur, snapped softly at his hand.

"How come that boy shot you in the back?" Junie Moon said. She was driving sixty miles an hour and the wind was whistling in through the windows and the cracks and breaking over the high radiator of the truck so that they could barely hear each other.

"Because I couldn't stop him," Warren said. He was feeling reckless and as though it would be fun to tease her, but he had no intention of telling her what had really happened.

"I know something about that feeling," she said. Her voice had a harshness to it that gave him goose pimples. "It's like having your feet stuck in the cement of an awful dream," she said.

Warren was miffed that she had turned the subject away from him. "Some things that happen are worse than the most frightful of dreams," he said, trying to sound mysterious.

"I couldn't agree with you more," she said. "How about stopping for a doughnut?"

Oh, Guiles, he thought, you would never turn me off that way.

"I hate doughnuts," Warren said.

She stopped the truck anyway, and after looking from one to the other of the men, she hopped out. The place was a Jazu Shoppe, one of a chain they had seen along the highway, all of them built the same way, with a neon Sultan out front, beckoning. "I may never get out alive," she said, winking at Warren, and as usual she restored his good spirits.

"That woman makes me so mad sometimes I could kill her," Warren said. His voice was as tender as a lover's voice.

Arthur bristled: "She is a fine woman, goddamn it."

"That's just what I said," Warren said. "The trouble, Arthur, with you is that you seldom listen to me, and when you do you don't hear, and when you do hear you hear wrong, and even when you hear right you change it so fast that it's never the same."

"I am going to die," Arthur said.

"Furthermore," Warren went on, "you put another person's suffering into your *will-call* file, to be examined only when your own ailments have been settled. And, furthermore, you are not going to die."

"I am so." Arthur sounded like a wounded child.

Arthur's words had chilled Warren because he knew that Arthur was right. That was why they were taking the vacation. That was why Mario had planned it all. That was why Junie Moon drove the truck so fast, her hands bleeding into the mitts Mario had made. It was as though if they got there and back fast enough or right enough or without driving over a thousand hidden cracks Arthur would not die. Warren was not an intuitive man, but the tendrils of his feelings sometimes extended beyond himself in extraordinary directions and to extraordinary depths. But, oddly enough, all he could think of at the moment was *The Conquest of Mexico*. The poor Mexican Indian is praying beside his water hole, Warren thought, pleading with the gods to emerge out of the mud—and all the while, just over the brow of the hill, the Spanish are waiting with their bright steel knives. Guiles, please come and help us.

A station wagon pulled alongside and a pale man with a carload of children looked bleakly at the beckoning Sultan. The children were thin and had snotty noses and tangled hair as though their mother had been dead for a long time.

"I don't want to have to tell you again," the father said, as though no sentence ever began without these words, "that when we get inside, you are to *listen* and to *behave*." A little boy of seven was sitting astride his younger sister, pinching her lips into painful silence. He belched in response to his father's remark.

"I don't like that group," Warren said. And, to his surprise, Arthur agreed.

"Sometimes I like you," Arthur said, and Warren, taken off guard, blushed and rolled down the window. "You've got a lot of class, Warren," Arthur continued. "You probably think I'm putting you on, but I wanted you to know I like your style." Arthur drew in his breath for the final compliment: "I'll bet that if you didn't have your paraplegia you'd be a regular Errol Flynn." With that he ducked down behind the seat and poked at the dog again.

Warren was scarlet with pleasure. This was the last thing he had expected from Arthur. In fact, it had been such a long time since he had gotten a compliment from anybody that he had begun to think it would never happen again. He did not trust himself to reply for a long time.

Finally he said something he had not intended to. "I think Junie Moon loves you, Arthur."

There was a thrashing from the back as Arthur sat up.

"What the hell are you talking about?" he said. "Why are you always going around spreading lies and rumors?" His hand banged against the back of the seat, and although Warren was irritated by him, he automatically reached over and held Arthur's trembling arm.

"I thought you told me I had style," Warren said.

"I take it back."

"You can't take back something that's true."

"She does not love me," Arthur said. "She loves Mario."

"Ho!" Warren shouted.

" 'Ho' is Junie Moon's word, damn it to hell."

Warren shrieked with laughter.

So they had both heard what they wanted to hear, but neither of them could listen to it.

Junie Moon came back to the truck with a Jazu Sultan cardboard container with coffee and doughnuts and something called Jazu's Pecan Delight and a Jazuburger with relish and onions for the dog. As she handed the container through the window to Warren, one of the thin, snotty-nosed children saw her.

"Look," she shouted, "it's the lady from outer space."

This brought them all running. Their father had disappeared into the Shoppe, probably glad to be rid of them. They advanced on her like a shambling, sullen army and stood a few feet away, staring.

"Get out of here," Warren yelled.

"That one's got a beard," the little girl said.

Her older brother jammed his hands in his pockets. "He's one of them stupid beatniks," he said.

"Beatnik, beatnik," said the smallest one, jumping up and down.

Warren opened the door to the truck and swung himself to the ground with his powerful arms. But he had forgotten that his wheelchair wasn't there, and there he hung, his thin legs folded across each other, the muscles as limp as reeds.

The boy, sensing an advantage, took a step closer.

"What's the matter, skinny legs, ya chicken?"

"Why don't you come over here and see," Warren said, his face red with anger. Without his chair to move in or a crutch to defend himself, he felt as helpless as a ripe plumb hanging on a tree.

"Get back in the truck," Junie Moon said to Warren. She did not like the look on the boy's face or the fact that a man and his wife who had come out of the Shoppe had stopped to stare.

"Is that the beatnik's mother?" said the smallest one, pointing to Junie Moon. She clapped her hand over her mouth and giggled through her fingers.

"For Christsakes, let's get out of here," Arthur said from the back of the truck.

A man with a red flowered shirt rounded the station wagon. "What's going on here?" he said.

"That man called me a dirty sonofabitch," the boy said, looking steadily into the man's eyes.

"Yes, he did! Yes, he did!" said the littlest girl.

Junie Moon got in the truck and started the engine.

"Just a damned minute," the man said. "I don't like the looks of none of this."

"Warren, for God's sake get in!" Junie Moon raced the engine.

"I can't," Warren hissed at her.

Arthur opened the back door and jumped to the ground. His leg was so weak he fell to one knee and his arm trembled as he tried to push himself to his feet.

"Where do you get off swearing at a little kid?" the man in the flowered shirt said. His eyes were small and close together and his short bristly hair was cut so that the top of his head looked hard and narrow.

"I didn't," said Warren, and he grabbed the side of the door and tried to pull himself back up into the cab.

"Why don't you mind your own damned business," Arthur said. He was standing now and he was not trembling and he was not even afraid that he would have a seizure. In fact, he wished the man would get nasty, because he felt like hitting him and showing off to Junie Moon.

"Look what came out from under a rock," the man said and he snickered to the children and the others who had gathered. With that the dog jumped out and walked slowly between the man and Arthur. He made a low rumbling noise in his throat and flattened his ears.

"I think I'll just go in and call the sheriff," the man said, glancing at the dog and walking off quickly toward the Shoppe. Arthur boosted Warren into the cab and jumped in after him. Junie Moon let out the clutch and they tore across the parking lot.

"You scared the hell out of him," Warren said to Arthur.

"Lordy yes," said Junie Moon. "You know, I've met a lot of rotten kids in my time, and they all have yellow eyes."

The truck bumped into the highway and for a while they rode in silence.

Finally Warren said: "I've got to invent a little folding

chair so I won't get caught like that again—dangling like a damned doll."

"You were both very gallant," Junie Moon said. "I feel like the queen of all ancient China."

"In my small, collapsible chair I will carry a switchblade knife, just in case," Warren said, "and a soupçon of tear gas." He held his hands out in front of him and the palms were bleeding.

"Jesus," Arthur said, giving him a handkerchief, "how did you do that?"

"Trying to pull myself into the truck." He winked at Arthur.

"Please don't wink at me," Arthur said.

"Why not?" said Junie Moon. "Why shouldn't he wink at you?"

"Because it makes me nervous," Arthur said.

"About what?"

"I don't know. It makes me think he's queer."

"So what if he is," Junie Moon said, nudging Warren in the ribs. "Winking is certainly inoffensive enough. You don't have to wink back."

"It would be friendlier if he did," Warren said, giggling. Warren did not like the sight of blood, least of all his own, and he was glad for a joke to take his mind off his hands. "Sometimes I conduct surveys," he continued. "When I go down the street, I wink at everyone I meet: man, woman, and child. Then I see how many wink back. More men than women wink back. Would you have guessed that? And practically all the children do. Of course, I surmise that the children who don't wink haven't yet learned to do so."

"You're always making excuses," Arthur said, smiling.

"Then along with the wink sometimes I make a little kissing motion. I can't begin to tell you how sexy that looks."

"No, please don't," Arthur said. "One day the Commissioner of Welfare and Decency will come and haul us off in a big black wagon."

"The sin patrol," said Junie Moon, "headed by Sidney Wyner."

"Oh Lord," Arthur said suddenly. "The dog!"

"Isn't he in the truck?" Warren said.

Arthur looked to be sure. "No. He got out when I did. We'll have to turn around."

But Junie Moon did not turn around. She did not even slow down. "He probably didn't want to come with us," she said. "Otherwise he would have gotten in."

"You'll have to go back," Arthur said.

But her face was impassive and she stared straight ahead at the highway. "I'm not going back there," she said. "There will only be trouble."

"You're kidding," Arthur said. "We can't just drive off and leave him."

"We can't?" She pushed down on the gas pedal.

Arthur's voice was shrill. "You stop the truck or I will open the door and jump out."

"See if I care," she said. "You like that damned dog more than you do . . ." Her voice trailed off but Warren would not let it go at that.

"More than he does whom?" Warren said. He liked the idea that this might be a lovers' quarrel, even though the participants were not aware of it. "It sounds like somebody I know is jealous," he said, and he winked at Junie Moon.

"Mind your own business," she said to him. "And stop winking!"

"That dog was trying to protect us and that's what he gets for it," Arthur said.

"Nobody asked him to protect us," Junie Moon said. "He's a tramp dog and all he knows is how to look after himself. He doesn't give one damn about you or anyone else."

"He sat with me out in the terrible sun that day when I almost died. He did that for me."

"He was tired, that's why he sat there. I can't stand people who try to make out that dogs do things for human reasons."

"My grandmother's Pekingese were said to have extrasensory powers and would forecast disaster by burying their heads in their paws for hours at a time," Warren said.

"That sounds like any old lazy dog's trick," Junie Moon said.

"You stop this goddamned truck!" Arthur screamed, and a tremor raged through his body which knocked him off the seat and onto the floor of the cab.

With this amount of persuasion, Junie Moon pulled off the road into a wayside park.

"If you won't go back," Arthur said, "we will wait here until he catches up." His lips were pale and trembling.

"We will wait here until the day of doom and we will never see that dog again," Junie Moon said.

"This time you are wrong," Arthur said. "And you know it."

Junie Moon took the food she had bought at the Jazu Shoppe and put it on the picnic table, but only Warren ate it. Warren had taken his wheelchair out of the truck and in a little while set off in it through the gentle woods to the side of a stream. He was able to get places in his chair that some people found difficult to navigate on foot. It was pleasant by the stream, and he sat there dreaming about his grandmother and her Pekingese and her biochemical ways. If you understand the composition of a thing, she had said in her brisk voice, you will be able to predict exactly what it will do. But that would take the fun out of it, he had objected. Silly boy, she had said, fun is more than a series of surprises. What is it, then? he had asked. But she had turned away, no doubt bent on another analysis. Had she known his composition, he wondered, and as a consequence predicted his destiny? He remembered her pursed lips and he smiled.

Arthur propped himself against the trunk of a pine tree so that he could see the road. He was angry and fearful—fearful that the dog might not come and angry because he had forgotten him and because he had meant nothing to Junie Moon. She was a hard, mean woman, he thought, who cared about nobody except perhaps that stupid fish peddler. She probably thought as much about the dog being lost as she had about me when I ran away. He watched her get back into the truck and sit behind the wheel as stiff as a ramrod. She was a dictator and heartless and ugly, ugly, ugly. She was no more like Ramona than the man in the moon. Ramona had big, soft legs and would have half killed him with her passion—if they had ever had the chance. Not that bony, ugly freak who sat there just waiting to drive off and leave *him* next.

"Don't get any damned ideas about leaving me," he called.

"Ho!" she shouted back at him.

Ramona would make love with him right there in the open if she had been along. She wouldn't have been afraid. And she would love the dog and feed him big hunks of meat instead of cornflakes.

Then, painfully, Arthur thought of his having revisited the state school the day he had run away. He remembered the painful heat and the guard's suspicious questions and finally slipping past the main building and rounding the corner where he could look into the window of the kitchen. The kitchen had been empty, cool, and smelling of soap and something simmering on a back burner. The chopping board stood where it had always been, and then his heart leaped, because he saw the knife Ramona had always used to slice and chop and beckon with. The knife she had de-pantsed him with. Could she still be there after all these years? "Ah, kiddo"—her voice remembered was strong and warm as she wiped his mouth with the back of her hand.

He had left that day without asking if she were still there. He could not get up his courage, even then.

I am going to join all the itchy-footed mamas, Junie Moon thought, who are sitting beside the ocean. I'm going to put this lousy truck in gear and leave them both here. I hope that rotten dog gets hit by a car and that those two die of starvation right here in this mangy wayside rest. I hope their bones bleach and blow away and that they don't even have a funeral. When Junie Moon finished having all these thoughts, she felt better. The trouble was she had never loved anybody much before so everything was set off at once, like the opening of a floodgate. And she did not want to love Arthur, because, as he himself would be the first to say, he had a progressive neurological disease. This was his polite way of saying he was dying.

About two hours later, Arthur had given up that the dog would come and Junie Moon had relented—to herself—and wished she had gone back for him. It was then the dog came loping down the road. To an outsider it would have looked as if the dog did not know them at all. He sniffed once, passed Arthur's outstretched hand, and peed on the back of the tree where Arthur was sitting. He then followed Warren's scent to the stream, ignored Warren's shout, dunked himself in the stream and trotted back. He then jumped up into the cab and shook himself vigorously, soaking Junie Moon and the seat of the truck.

"It served you right," Arthur shouted, and laughing, he took the hamburger off the table and fed it, piece by piece, to the dog.

Nineteen

They drove another day until the signs of the sea began—scrub pine and sand and motels with names like The Driftwood and Vista del Mar. The dog slept most of the time lying on his back with his legs in the air as straight as sticks. Once in a while he would look at Junie Moon and growl.

For Junie Moon and Warren the vacation was like The Great Escape. She drove too fast, weaving in and out of highway traffic with a calculated recklessness which Warren admired. And Warren saw himself on another exotic brink, about to turn the page to Adventure.

"I have decided that we will stay at Patty's Hideaway," Warren said. He had watched the billboards and had been particularly persuaded by one of them which read: *Come and Frolic with the Stars.*

"I wonder if you can pick your star?" Junie Moon said as she swung the truck out smartly to pass a Volkswagen.

In these hours Junie Moon and Warren were each other's oldest friend.

"I have always wanted to be rich and to be in love," Warren said.

"You give up your freedom on both counts," Junie Moon said, leaning hard on the horn.

"You do not!" Warren said. "Love is warming."

"Ahhhhh," she said.

"Love is rejuvenating!" he said.

"Is that a fact?"

"It's the living end."

"I would have to agree with you there," she said, and she stepped on the gas and tore through a narrow opening between two trucks.

"It seems like we have been living together for a long time," Warren said.

"Is that good or bad?" she said.

He laughed. "I don't know, but it's a relief. I've known too many pantries and spare rooms. *Our* house seems quite elegant." The sun was shining directly in the window, so it was hard to tell if he were really blushing or not.

In the back of the truck Arthur listened and tried to understand why such a sweet feeling should be so edged with pain.

"I wouldn't call it elegant," Arthur said.

"Another country heard from," said Warren.

By now it was impossible for Warren and Arthur to talk without arguing. The sting had gone out of it, but it was a habit—as though they were an old, carping couple married for years.

"Why are you always talking about love?" Arthur said.

Warren laughed. In his mind he had spun a golden dream of himself in a thousand exotic poses with arm-banded slaves and tender young women lining the royal bath. Soft winds played around the edges of the palace, and in the jasmine the Chinese nightingale cried, "Darling, darling!"

"It just so happens," he said, "that I am not ashamed of love or loving. That is a testimony to my maturity."

"Ho!" said Junie Moon, braking the truck with such violence that the dog banged his head against the back of the front seat.

Arthur surprised himself. "You and your 'ho'! As if that makes you an expert!"

Junie Moon scowled and noted that a number of bugs, probably grasshoppers, had been smashed against the windshield.

"My advice to you," she said, "is not to fly along the highway."

"What?" said Arthur.

"Especially if you happen to be a grasshopper," she said.

Arthur stretched out so that he could see the back of her head. The dog put his muzzle close to Arthur's ear and made little wheezing noises as if he were telling him something sweet and unimportant.

"Good old dog," Arthur said.

"What did you say?" Junie Moon said.

Arthur smiled. "Nothing that would interest you." He looked at her semi-profile, and because he was not bothered any more by her terrible scars, he felt he had a special right to her. As yet he could not admit that this might be love.

Patty's Hideaway was a big jazzy hotel crushed in between two other big jazzy hotels and with a few feet of
beach front. But it had palms, said Warren, and a swimming
pool, and he would get them rooms which overlooked the
sea.

"How are you going to do that?" Junie Moon said.

"Never mind how," he said. "I've been planning it all the
way down. But you have to play the game."

"What game?" Mysterious things like this made Arthur
nervous.

"All you have to do," Warren said testily, "is pretend to
be important. I'll do the rest."

"How do we do that?" Arthur said.

"Just keep your mouth shut and try to look bored."

He made them stop a block from the hotel, where he
changed his shirt for a soft pink and purple striped beach
jacket, combed his beard, and finally arranged himself in his
wheelchair, a silver-headed cane across his lap. He gave
them a wicked laugh and wheeled off down the street, looking like some crazy Italian prince.

"I am afraid of hotel lobbies," Junie Moon said, watching
him go.

"So am I," said Arthur. "I am always sure my underwear
will fall out of the suitcase." He bent over and touched her
shoulder, and then, as usual, he said what he had not meant
to say: "How come you drove off and left the dog behind?"

"The dog will have to stay in the truck and guard it," she
said, ignoring his question and looking out the window.
"Patty's Hideaway probably does not allow dogs."

"He could have starved to death or burst his heart trying

to catch up with us." Arthur could not stop pursuing this awful line of accusation. It was like his being stuck in the Western Union office when Sam wouldn't give him a job.

Junie Moon stretched and slumped down behind the steering wheel. "Did you know that dogs like to have jobs— at least male dogs. They like to fetch and run and police."

"That was a terrible, terrible thing, leaving him," said Arthur.

"Female dogs, on the other hand, prefer to sit and dream of other days." Arthur's face was almost touching her own now and she pushed him away. "I did stop the truck, finally," she said.

"But only after I fell on the floor!" he shouted.

"Perhaps I would have stopped anyway."

"How do I know that?"

"You don't. And you won't. You won't ever know that, so shut up about it." She looked at him and winked and he had to smile.

"Help me get out of these damned bloody mittens," she said.

As he pulled the mittens off her hands, being as careful as he could not to hurt her more, he suddenly winked back.

"I'd better look out," she said. "You might be queer."

Warren had worked his magic with Patty's Hideaway. He never told them exactly how, partly because he wished to be able to elaborate on it later and partly because he had certain trade secrets he preferred to keep to himself. At any rate, in a little while he returned with a uniformed doorman who drove the truck to a side entrance where they were met by the manager and two attendants and whisked through the lobby with Junie Moon being treated as though she were Garbo or royalty from a small country. The dog followed, almost peed on the side of the door, then changed his mind and came along, his tail high in the air as if he were some elegant and ancient breed.

Warren tipped the manager fifty dollars as though it were nothing, and Arthur tried his best to look bored and keep his mouth shut. There was no mention of their lack of baggage and the shopping bags were placed discreetly to one side and then Warren dismissed them with a bored wave of his hand.

When the door had been shut, Arthur and Junie Moon began to giggle, but not Warren. He looked down his nose at them as if he had found them on the street. The truth was, he was now the real Italian prince and he had no intention of undermining himself.

Beach Boy had seen them go through the lobby. He was chatting with a bellhop, getting the low-down on who had checked in—which ones were available, which ones had money, which ones were looking for a good time. Beach Boy was red-brown and gleamed in the sun. He had all the right attributes for his job: his legs were long and slender, he had fine hands, and, as if this weren't enough, he had a quick white-toothed smile and hair that cowlicked back from his forehead. He had been raised in the foothills by a group of relatives where no one in particular took care of him. This resulted in his being restless and somewhat of a dreamer, and he took long walks on the beach gathering things. When he grew older, the fat ladies on the beach began to admire his shells and invite him to their rooms for further inspection. He found that he could make a rather good living by pretending not to know what they were talking about but at the same time touching them gently here and there and innocently begging their pardon.

By the time he was seventeen he was hired by the hotel to smooth out the sand and set up the umbrellas and in other ways be helpful to the guests.

When Beach Boy first saw Warren and Junie Moon and Arthur, he was not repulsed by what he saw because he had never seen anything like them before. They were also a pleasant change from the fat women with their charm bracelets and sly grins.

"Hey man, see what I see," he said to the bellhop. Beach Boy was inarticulate in a number of languages, with the result that his speech sounded sweet and musical.

"Somebody going incognito," the bellhop said sagely. Beach Boy felt his day improve immediately, although he did not know why, exactly. He pushed his white duck pants dangerously low on his hips and ran his hand reflectively over his golden chest. "Ahhh," he said, and the muscles over his belly rippled as if by instinct.

The dog stood with his nose high, sniffing the sea air as if it were some long-forgotten perfume. Then he drank long and lustily from the toilet bowl and stretched out on the bed in Junie Moon's room, his head on the pillow. She threw a shoe at him, but he did not move.

They had two rooms connected by a balcony and facing the sea. Below, to the right, was the swimming pool, looking somewhat smaller than it had on the billboards, but inviting enough, with a springboard and rubber rafts and music piped over the loudspeaker. Only a few people swam in the sea.

"I'm going out and look around," Warren said, and he wheeled away before they could say a word.

Junie Moon sat on the balcony. The crowd of people below distressed her, but she was glad she was there nonetheless. It had been a long time since she had felt in any way festive. She closed her eyes and imagined she could hear the sound of the sea over the music.

Arthur thought: the sick feeling will pass. All you have to do is lie down for a while and do a chess problem in your head.

"I'm going to lie down for a while," he said to Junie Moon, but she did not answer him. He pulled the shutters against the light and heard the roar beginning in his ears, like the sound of wings. Don't forget, he thought, that the queen's pawn is the queen's favorite and as such has special talents. He also has certain weaknesses, probably because of bad blood brought on by the marriage of cousins. Maybe the pawn is really the queen's illegitimate son.

Arthur rolled onto his stomach and held the bed with his outstretched arms. Once when he was a child he had gone through the Tunnel of Horrors at an amusement park. He had been strapped into a seat on what looked like a railroad flatcar, and with a great wrenching screech the car tore off into a pitch-black tunnel. *Let me out*, he had cried, *let me out*, and he heard a man behind him laugh. There were pulsing, electronic noises in the tunnel, which were loud and

undulating like brain waves, and the rhythm seemed syn-
chronized with his own personal rhythm to such an extent
that he felt himself falling into a seizure. By the time the
train emerged from the other end of the ghastly tunnel, the
seizure had passed and Arthur leaned against the seat belt
pale and sick. "How about that, sonny?" the man sitting behind had shouted. "How about that for a good scare?"

The queen's pawn was her lover, not her illegitimate son.
That's why he rushed out so quickly—and so blindly?—to
defend her. How about *that*, queenie old girl? How about
that for a stellar defense? Tell me that you love me, tell me
that you'll kiss me, tell me that you'll miss me, queenie mine.
Let me out! Let me out!

"Are you all right in there?" Junie Moon called.

"Yes!" He buried his head in the pillow so she would not
hear his sobs. He could not believe that he was developing
the worst symptom of all.

At three o'clock Warren telephoned from the lobby and
told them to come down. "The Beach Boy has fixed us a
place," he said, "just for us. Take number 3 elevator.
They've been told to pick up only you."

Junie Moon knocked on Arthur's door. "Come on," she
said. "Let's go frolic with the stars."

Arthur raised his head and decided he could make it.

Beach Boy had dragged Warren's wheelchair through the
sand and spread out towels and erected two bamboo screens
for privacy. He stared frankly at Junie Moon, not in any
superior, rude way, but because he had never seen a woman
whose face and hands looked as though they had been

blasted off. She winked at him, and he blinked in surprise and then burst out in a laugh.

"Welcome to Patty's Hideaway," and he took her hand without a pause and helped her into the chaise.

As Arthur stretched out on the sand, he had a particularly violent spasm in his arm. "Wow, man!" Beach Boy said, looking at Arthur with admiration.

But, of the three, Beach Boy liked Warren the best. When he had finished arranging things, he turned to Warren. "Okay, captain?" he said.

Warren flushed with pleasure.

"You like to go out to the reef with me?" Beach Boy said to Warren.

Warren could only nod. He thought that if he tried to say anything to this beautiful red-brown man he would burst into tears.

"He will not go out to the reef with you—or anybody else, for that matter," Junie Moon said.

"Why not?" Beach Boy said.

"Because he can't swim a damned stroke."

"No matter," Beach Boy said, and with that he leaned down and threw Warren over his beautiful shoulders and carried him to the water's edge. There he placed him gently on his black surfboard, arranging Warren's thin legs as though they were of fragile porcelain. The water dripped golden from his back as he pushed the board through the surf. Then with an easy leap he was on the board behind Warren. The board jumped as he made the first stroke. Warren joined him in the stroking with his own twice-powerful arms and the board knifed like a porpoise.

Arthur thought: I am better now, but it won't last. I must tell her quickly what I feel. Instead he said: "How come Warren finds such good-looking people?"

"I don't know," Junie Moon said. "He loves the excitement and the seducing and being seduced and all of those beginning things."

"So do I," Arthur said abruptly. At last he had kicked a hole in his own dam. He moved closer to her and patted a mound of sand into breast shapes. The roar of wings had passed for the moment.

"Is that a fact," she said, staring out beyond the breakers.

"And furthermore," he said, placing a pebble in the center of each mound, "I happen to know that you are not tough, like you pretend to be."

"Have you been consulting the soothsayer?" she said.

"I am capable of making my own observations," he said, shaping a long fat belly in the sand beneath the breasts, "even though I may not give that appearance." He was shaken by a tremor and the sand figure was scattered and gone.

Junie Moon put her hand on him as she always did, and she wondered if his thin bones felt different to her or whether it was only her imagination.

Arthur drew in his breath and said quickly, before he lost his nerve: "I love you. What do you think of that?"

"I don't know," Junie Moon said after a while, "because you are asking me to react to how *you* feel, and how in the world could I do that? As for me, I haven't loved anybody in a long time. I've gotten rusty and forgetful, among other things."

"You are certainly making a long enough speech," Arthur

said, and he gave her one of his rare grins which almost made him look young.

"In the past, when somebody said they loved me, I always felt obligated to love them back. I succeeded too, without trying too hard. Do you think that was insincere of me?"

"Your speech gets longer and longer the more you talk," Arthur said.

"I never really believed them, anyway," Junie Moon said, pulling her hat over her eyes until her face was barely visible. "They went on and on as if they were reading directions on how to put together a model airplane. They sounded logical too, if you bothered to listen. Mostly the formula was the same: they hadn't expected to fall in love, but lo and behold there they were, and if I would only do this or that, their miserable lives would be complete."

"The trouble is," Arthur said, "I am about as helpless as I look. There would be very few surprises."

"So I would do this or that and then the fun would die down and we would be left with each other," she said. "That of course is the hard part."

"I am almost a virgin," Arthur said, "so I wouldn't know."

"Once I went out with a man named Stanley Adams," she said. "He came from Tulsa, Oklahoma, once upon a time, but he had become a short-order cook and traveled around the countryside getting jobs and quitting them. He had bad teeth."

"I have teeth like rocks," Arthur said, baring them at her.

"One day Stanley Adams said, 'Junie Moon, I never thought I'd say this, but I love you.' Now what kind of a beginning is that, I ask you?"

"It's true," Arthur said, "that over the years two of my teeth have been extracted."

"He was a miserable man in other ways," she said. "He hemmed and hawed a lot, but he was also crude and to the point. He used a very vulgar term, as I recall."

"When I was young, my teeth were even stronger," he said. "I could crack walnuts with them."

"The term that offended me was *let's shack up*. Not the idea of doing it but of doing it in a shack bothered the hell out of me. You could just bet that Stanley Adams never did it in any place other than a shack. Lordy!"

"I have done it very little any place, if at all," he said.

" 'How about it?' he would say. Arthur, I hope you never say 'How about it' to me."

"I wish you wouldn't talk about Stanley Adams."

"Why not?"

"I don't know, but it makes everything sound sad."

"Are you jealous of Stanley Adams?"

"Yes."

"Well, don't be. In addition to having bad teeth, he had dandruff which extended out of his hairline to the tops of his ears."

"You never miss a thing when it comes to observing a man," Arthur said. "I must watch myself at all times."

They sat in silence for a long time. Junie Moon pulled her sombrero over her eyes and he could not tell anything about what she was feeling.

"Do you see those birds flying?" he said at last, pointing to a cloud of terns wheeling in the sky. "They roost in the mangroves."

She did not reply. Arthur thought: Tell me all there is to

tell about you. About the day you were born, about everything except old lovers, but of every other joy. Tell me about other times, about the things you wanted most in those days.

"By roosting in the mangroves," he said, "they are near the source of their breakfast."

He thought: I wish I were rich and famous and could say here I am, a prize for you! Some prize! Give me a tiny clue, some shred of your thoughts. Tell me that you like me, love me, tell me that you don't hate me, tell me.

"They apparently eat the small fishes who live among the mangrove roots," he said.

"Let's go back," she said.

Warren was sunburned and salty and could not shut up.

"Guiles is taking me to a party tonight."

"Guiles?" Junie Moon snorted.

Warren reddened. "Beach Boy doesn't mind if I call him that. I loved Guiles and I loved his name and there has never been anyone else I knew with that name so that I could call it."

"It sounds silly, if you ask me," Arthur said.

"I have better sense than to ask you anything," Warren snapped.

"Hush!" Junie Moon said, and they stopped fighting.

"He took me downtown in his jeep," Warren said happily. "He had to buy some things for the party tonight. I sat in the jeep and waited for him. Wasn't that nice?"

"Ducky," said Arthur.

"Ahhhhh," Junie Moon warned.

"I saw the most darling little group," Warren said. "They were walking down the street together—a little tiny lady and her daughter. The daughter was carrying a dog. All three of them were albinos."

"You're a liar," Arthur said. He wished Warren would go on to his damned party and leave him alone with Junie Moon. He ached for the privacy to look at her and to try again to tell her what he felt.

"And then we went to a fancy men's store and Guiles bought a pair of red and white stripped bathing trunks. I loaned him the money. As a matter of fact, I insisted he take it. The trunks were perfect on him."

"You loaned him *our* money?" Arthur was furious.

"Of course. I considered it a good investment. At first he thought I was after him because he was so darned good-looking. Now he knows better and has planned my days for the rest of our time here."

Junie Moon laughed. "I wouldn't mind if somebody loved me for my money."

"There are a lot of rich people that Guiles has to look after. He showed me a man today on the beach with his mongoloid son. The son was about forty years old and looked mushy and white and the man was rubbing sun-tan oil on him. Guiles has to take the son on the surfboard, but not out to the reef like he took me."

Arthur thought: I wish I had loved her right from the beginning. Now so many days are lost and gone.

"And sometimes, so he says, he has to entertain rich old women who come down here all by themselves or whose husbands spend the day sleeping under an umbrella. He's going to show me one."

"How does he do that?" said Junie Moon.

Arthur thought: She can make her voice as thick as honey when she wants to.

"You don't think I asked him *that*, do you?" Warren giggled.

"You certainly did," Junie Moon said, "and he told you in excruciating detail."

There was a knock and Beach Boy stood smiling in the doorway. He wore clean white ducks and an unbuttoned shirt and no shoes.

"Ah, captain, you ready?" And to Junie Moon: "Don't you worry, I take care of *him*."

"I'm not his mother," she said.

Beach Boy laughed. "No?" and with this he swung Warren over his shoulder.

"You can see why he would remind me of Guiles," Warren said as they went out the door.

When the door had closed, Junie Moon turned abruptly to Arthur. Her eyes looked hard, but when she spoke, her voice had the uncertainty of too much feeling.

"Look, Arthur," she said, "I'm not so tough as you think I thought I was."

"I know it," he said. He was overcome by such a passionate shyness that he had to turn his head.

"And furthermore," she said, "you may not have thought that I was listening, but I heard every word you said today on the beach."

"That's good." Calm your heart first, he thought, or it may have its own private fit and die.

"I am perfectly aware that terns roost in the mangroves," she said, smiling. But this time there was none of her usual sarcasm. "And that they enjoy eating the fishes who live nearby."

He thought: If I touch her, we will both be blown to kingdom come.

"I wish to God you would hug me and shut up about your nature lecture," he said. She turned away from him because for the first time in many weeks she was acutely aware of how her face must look to another person.

The dog, who earlier had been fed two hamburgers and a bowl of spaghetti, watched this curious change of events from the bed he had appropriated. Once or twice he let out a deep sigh, but finally, when neither of them paid the slightest attention to him, he rolled over and lay in his favorite position with his legs straight in the air.

Warren did not come back to the hotel for three days. Instead, he went to a party that lasted that long. On Beach Boy's shoulder, he went first to see a fat blond lady who spoke baby-talk and who every year rented a house on the beach for a month and who, every third night or so, paid Beach Boy a large sum to come and bring his friends and drink and dance with her. She sat in the middle of the living-room floor, surrounded by men (early in this arrangement she had told him not to bother to bring women—they made her nervous), while a phonograph played continually and a maid served cold lobster and big pots of cheese and caviar and kept the glasses full. One by one the boys would get up and dance with the woman until she would have to rest because of exhaustion. They would hold her close in their strong arms and she would wiggle against them like a silly twelve-year-old pretending to be sexy. The young men did not really have a good time, but they came because of the fine food and drink and the oddity of it. Later in the evening they would go find their own girls and show them what sex was all about.

When Beach Boy arrived with Warren, the fat blonde scowled, but he paid no attention. He kicked a big pillow onto the floor and placed Warren on it as if this were a present for her. Warren gave her one of his big sweet grins and that melted her and for the next few hours she talked with him and didn't dance at all.

About two in the morning Warren got hoisted up again and he and Beach Boy drove to the side entrance of the local dance hall. Beach Boy chose three girls from those who didn't belong to anyone at the moment and they drove out to a lonely stretch of beach and lay in a circle under the stars. A little later Beach Boy told one of the girls that she was to stay with Warren and look after him while he and the other two walked a discreet distance away to make love. Before he left, he put a bottle of twenty-five-year-old Scotch and a jar of caviar next to Warren. "Just in case, captain," he said, laughing. The girl waited about forty-five seconds, and before Warren could even begin to get nervous, she was on him and doing things he would never have imagined, even in his wildest dreams.

As the sun came up, they went farther out of town to a ramshackle diner near the pier where they all ate enough food for ten men. The girls went home then, but Beach Boy went to the hotel and got his surfboard and they drove to another beach tucked behind a high cliff. Beach Boy carried the board down first and then came back for Warren. They took off their clothes and headed the big board out to sea and for the next three hours they lay sunning themselves like a couple of fat seals.

"Life is a dream," Arthur said, and he held her close to him and looked out to the sea.

"It's not life but love that's the dream," Junie Moon said. "If by a dream you mean something that's sweeter."

"Life is sweeter now," he said. "Before there were only signs and symptoms and tracts and plaques and reflexes that had long since gone sour. Would you care to dance?"

Below, the music played softly over the loudspeaker. They stood close together and danced without either of them moving very much.

"I didn't say 'How about it' to you, did I?" He laughed.

"Thank God."

"And I didn't say, 'Let's shack up' either. Did I?"

"You didn't have to. We did that long ago."

He sighed so deeply it sounded like a moan. "Once I saw a peach tree that was dying."

"Hush."

"It was past the season and it did a very foolish thing."

"Tell me another time."

"All the other trees were bare, but this dying tree suddenly put out a full crop of leaves and peaches."

She felt him tremble and she held him close to her.

"You talk too much."

"The trouble was," he said, "the peaches didn't taste like peaches."

"That was because it was late in the season and you expected too much of them."

"Maybe," he said. "For a mean woman, you say a lot of smart things."

"You look tired," she said.

"Tell me everything there is to tell," he said, sitting down.

She lay next to him on the bed and smoothed his hair. "That would take about ten minutes," she said. "People are less complicated than you think."

"Then please begin." He closed his eyes, not to listen better but to try to fight off the dream of drowning that now seemed just around the corner.

She began: "My daddy was reported to have jumped up and down in front of the drugstore the day I was born. No one knew for sure why he did such a thing, but my grandmother, who was a cynical old soul and prone to speak her mind, speculated that the act of procreation had gone to his head. . . ."

The cloud of birds wheeled and dipped over the dark water crying in anger as if their nests had been ripped apart. Terns had been known to attack men, Arthur thought, and peck out their eyes. I must keep my chest expanded so that the air can flow in. In this way I can keep them from driving me into the sea.

"My grandmother always referred to him as 'that damn fool son of mine.' But not entirely without love. 'That damn fool son of mine bought a new car,' she would say proudly to the neighbors . . ."

Terns do not roost in peach trees, Arthur. Any damn fool knows they prefer mangroves.

"I suppose that a little boy who has been called a damned fool long enough begins to act like one . . ."

The respiration rate of a normal male is eighteen per minute, and his pulse is seventy, or approximately four times his respiration. On the other hand, birds have a very rapid pulse and must eat enormous amounts to keep alive.

"All my father ever wanted to do in this world was to take a trip to Yellowstone National Park. He never shut up about it and my mother would never agree to go . . ."

The throats of birds are too small for tracheotomy tubes. And besides, they are too nervous.

" 'Why you want to go to Yellowstone National Park when we can go to the ocean is beyond me,' my mother would say. Year after year. Arthur, are you all right?"

"Don't stop talking," he said, trying to smile. Her eyes were sad and he knew she was pretending not to notice that he was in trouble.

The queen moves forward and from side to side but she always sends her pawn out to do her dirty work. Now then, queen's pawn to queen's pawn four. Chessmen are better than birds. More reliable. And they have no respiration rate at all.

"I must take you to a doctor," she said after a while.

"No."

"You look pale."

"I am as strong as a bull."

"The hell you are. Maybe a doctor could give you something."

"Like what?"

"I don't know, Arthur. For Christssake, I don't know."

There were tears in her eyes and he looked away. "Take me home," he said. "Back to the banyan tree."

"But Warren isn't back yet."

"When he comes. I'll be all right until he comes."

"How about it if I take you to a doctor in the meantime?"

"*How about it?*" He managed to grin at her. "*How about it? You* using that dirty term with *me?*" He put his hand on her arm and she felt the tired weight of it. "When Warren comes, we will go home," she said.

Warren came the next day. He was brown and proud and sick with exhaustion. His main worry had been that Arthur and Junie Moon would not believe the truth about what had happened to him—it sounded so much like the lies he always told. When he wheeled into the room, he saw two things: that Arthur was in bad trouble and that he and Junie Moon had fallen in love or something like that. At first this made him panic because in any event he was bound to lose them. And then he was angry because they would not be in the mood to listen to his lively account of his days and nights with Beach Boy. Damn, damn, damn! He wanted to turn around and wheel out of the room and find Beach Boy again and never think about Arthur or that woman—hadn't he been forewarned that including her was a mistake?—he would make a life with this golden man and it would be like Provincetown, only warmer and sexier and farther away.

If he stayed, he would be taken again to the fat lady's house, and perhaps to the beach with the dance-hall girl. But how often to the reef on Beach Boy's surfboard? If he thought about it, Warren must say that Beach Boy had yellow eyes—yellow and never still—and it would be only a matter of time until there was trouble.

So he said to them, "I guess we've done everything there is to do here. How about going home?"

Twenty

Beach Boy helped them. He got the truck and brought it to the side door, and he carried Arthur down and arranged him as comfortably as possible in the back. He found a bowl of clam stew for the dog, and he took only a little money from Warren, with which he said he would pay their hotel bill. Warren winked at him over this, and Beach Boy winked back—the most delightful, charming wink that Warren had ever seen.

"Man, you take care," he said to Arthur. He swatted at the dog and he kissed Junie Moon on the back of the neck and then, with Warren, he just put his hands on his hips and looked Warren in the eye.

"Goodbye, baby," he said. "You come back any time. Guiles look after you."

It was almost a thousand miles they had to go. Warren tied the mitts over Junie Moon's hands, and she pulled her sombrero over her eyes like a cowboy riding on a cold windy mountain, and turned the truck out into the highway, keeping the gas pedal as close to the floorboards as she dared.

The dog lay down next to Arthur with his nose a few inches from Arthur's mouth, staring at him as if Arthur were about to speak the secrets of the past. And Warren chattered, not about the things he wanted to tell, but about little light bits of this and that which he felt would not offend or irritate. Like the dog, he hovered, for once keeping his presence as easy as possible.

For Junie Moon, the time had come to feel something. And the pain was more than anything she felt while she had been in the hospital. It was deeper than any fissure from the acid burns; it was more acrid than any seared and missing joint; and it was more wistful than pain receding. A silly, unlikely man who trembled at the slightest breath, who raged and ranted like a leaf tossed in the wind—the most unlikeliest of all—had touched her. And yet the thing that upset her the most was that she was not sure it was love.

But she drove like a demon, tailing the highballing trucks like they were emissaries of witches, flying through the dark night, past the EAT signs and the BLUE MOON MOTELS and the JAZU SHOPPES with the Sultans beckoning, beckoning. Warren never shut up.

"Don't stop talking to me," she said, and he took this for a compliment and then revealed things that were even little known to him.

Like: "I think that I am only capable of loving beautiful people. Melvin Coffee was the first one."

"And who, might I ask, was Melvin Coffee?"

"The boy who shot me in the back."

Junie Moon had swerved wildly to miss a farmer who had pulled his truck full of fat hogs into the highway in front of her.

"My mistake," Warren continued after a while, "was in telling him what I felt."

"It was not a mistake that you said it but that you told it to Melvin Coffee," she said.

The first dawn came sick and damp as they tore through a little puky town called Heavenly Peace.

"I'm going to stop here and get food. You climb in the back and feed it to Arthur as we go along."

"All right," said Warren.

She bought hot coffee and some special peanut-butter crackers Arthur liked. "Now don't anybody worry me," she said. "We are going straight home from here and we will only be stopping for gas, and it is a long, long way." Then she leaned over the steering wheel and set her eyes on the road in front of her and drove this way for almost twenty-three hours.

There was a faint streak of gray in the sky when they arrived. The wind had died out, leaving the dampness hanging in the air.

"We're home," she said. And then to Warren: "You've got to help me get him in."

"If I can," Warren said, trying to quiet the terrible trembling that fear had set off in him. He pulled himself over the seat into the back of the truck, where Arthur was lying. "We made it," he said. "You're going to be all right now." The dog's ears were flat against his head and he was looking the other way as though someone were yelling at him. Arthur opened his eyes and smiled.

"What time is it?" he said.

"Four o'clock," Warren said.

Junie Moon opened the back door of the truck. "Hurry," she whispered, and Warren scooted across the floorboards dragging Arthur with him.

"I'll try to walk," Arthur said. They put him gently on the ground. He put an arm around Junie Moon's shoulder and in this way they went up the path together.

"Put me under the tree," he said.

"Not on your life," she said, starting to the back door with him.

"Please, please."

So she put him down on the cot and covered him with blankets Warren brought from the truck.

"Go into the kitchen," she said to Warren.

"No," he said. "I can't."

"Go anyway," she said.

"I'm afraid," Warren said.

"I don't care what you are. You go into that kitchen. And if you're afraid, make some brownies."

"At this time of the morning?" But he went off, slamming the door behind him.

Arthur moaned. The dog lay down nearby, his head on his paws and his eyes narrow slits.

"Did you feed him?" Arthur said.

"Yes. Two hamburgers, and now he's developed a liking for pork and beans."

"You're teasing."

"No."

There was a soft flap of wings as the owl settled above them, followed by the little shower of leaves and twigs.

"He brought us luck," Arthur whispered.

"Old hooty owl did that all right."

"I meant the dog. Are you sorry you drove off and left him?"

"Yes."

Then Arthur shrieked as he tried to get his breath. "Hold me, hold me! I'm drowning."

"Yes, I'll hold you. I'll hold your head."

She pulled him up from the blankets and rested his head on her breast. She could hear the wild beating of his heart and the whine of air as it passed through the narrowing channel into his lungs.

"It's like the dream," he said.

"No," she said, "it is not like the dream." She patted his hair with her terrible fingers and he began to relax. "I won't let you die. You're too damned important to me."

"You're a liar," he said, turning into her like a child. He was growing soft in her arms and she was stricken by a panic so deep she could barely move. He's going bad, she thought, remembering the term they used in the hospital. Something vital had stopped working, like his kidneys or his lungs. She would have to do something, but she didn't know what. Then, instinctively, she turned him over her knees and, with his head hanging down, whacked him between the shoulder blades. There was a great gush and the blood rushed from his mouth and lay in a pool on the ground.

"Oh, my God," she said.

He raised his head and looked at her. His face was drained of all color but his eyes were as bright as a child's.

"I feel better," he said. "The wind has come up again. I can hear it in the banyan tree. It will be all right now."

She could barely see him through her tears.

"Thank you for keeping me from drowning," he said.

Then he lay back and smiled and in a matter of seconds he was dead.

◆ *Twenty-One*

Mario made all the arrangements. They went to the cemetery in the truck and the dog rode in the back. Afterwards Mario took them to his house and made them drink whiskey and eat hot bread and fresh butter. He told them that they were going to come and live with him now because he was sick to death of being alone.

"I will do nothing of the kind," said Junie Moon.

"And if *she* will do nothing of the kind," said Warren, "*I* too will not do it either."

Mario sighed. A little later he took them back to the house under the banyan tree. He went in and packed up everything he could find while Warren and Junie Moon sat outside and stared past each other.

"You should try for once not to be so bossy," Warren said finally.

"Look who is talking," she snapped.

"Arthur wouldn't have wanted it."

The explosion came then, and Sidney Wyner, who was peering through the hedge, had no difficulty whatsoever hearing her.

"You've got some goddamned nerve speaking for Arthur!" she yelled. "You just leave him out of this. People use that dumb expression when they want to get their own way. You of all people trying to tell *me* what *he* would have said! How would *you* know?"

"Because," Warren said in a whisper, "he was my friend too."

Mario shut the door to the kitchen and put on a new strong padlock he had taken from his pocket. Then he took Junie Moon's arm and led her to the truck. The dog sat under the tree and wouldn't move, so after Mario had gotten Warren in the truck, he picked up the dog and threw him in behind them.

"I know your type," he said to the dog, "and don't you forget it."